Sandy Cove - A Drake Wines Novella

Drake Wines, Volume 1.5

Chelle pimblott

Published by Chelle pimblott, 2021.

This is a work of fiction. Similarities to real people, places, or events are entirely coincidental.

SANDY COVE - A DRAKE WINES NOVELLA

First edition. May 19, 2021.

Copyright © 2021 Chelle pimblott.

Written by Chelle pimblott.

DEDICATION

To my book bitches without you I wouldn't be writing xx

To my editor in chief, thank you for all that you do and it goes way beyond editing and being a sounding board. Love ya guts!

To my family, thank you for allowing me to write and forgetting to cook for you sometimes. Love you always xx

****

***Please note ***

SANDY COVE

was written by an Australian Author, in Australian English.

As such you may assume there are some spelling errors within, however it's just how we spell things downunder.

****

Chapter One
SAMANTHA

I'll never forget the feeling I had that day, walking from my bungalow at the back of the resort, into the office and knowing that I was the one in charge. Pushing through the staff entrance, I knew I was wearing the biggest, goofiest grin possible, but I couldn't have hidden my happiness even if I'd wanted to. The resort was all mine to run. I earned my new position, having worked my way up from cleaning rooms, to work side by side with Bettie, and when she told me a few months ago that she'd met the man of her dreams and they were getting married, I was over the moon happy for her. Then she dropped her bombshell, she was going to retire, and they were moving further out on the island, and I feared the worst. I thought that she would sell the resort and I would be working for someone new that I would have to prove myself all over again.

As luck would have it, Bettie didn't sell the resort, she handed the reins over to a manager instead. Someone that she'd taken under her wing and taught everything she knew about the business and life. I'm grateful for the opportunity and the confidence Bettie has in me to do the job she recently gave up for love.

I felt like I was walking on air, and then Bettie asked to talk to me for a minute and my entire world got turned upside down and inside out, because that's when she told me she wanted to bring someone in to help me. Not because she thought I couldn't do it, but because she didn't want me to become the workaholic that she had, and she wanted me to enjoy being young and to find love. I'll remember that conversation until my dying breath.

"Bettie, you don't need to worry about me and my love life, or lack thereof. I promise." I said, smiling like a crazy person. I wasn't looking for love and I sure wasn't going to let it get in the way of me running this place.

"It's no bother sweetheart, trust me. You're going to like this guy. He's great. He's got experience and he'll balance you perfectly." She says with a dismissive wave of her hand, as if she doesn't realise that she just broke my heart. "I've been searching for the right person to be your right hand, and I'm so excited that I found him."

"I don't need a right or a left hand Bettie, I know the resort inside out and upside down."

She looks at me for the first time since I entered the office, which is now technically mine, but she's sitting behind the desk that's been hers for the last decade. "I know you don't necessarily need any help Samantha, but everyone needs a right hand man, an assistant manager. Someone to help with the day to day stuff, and I know that Tomas is going to be yours."

I took the sheet of paper she was handing me, because that's what you do when people hand you things. You take them. "What's this?"

"That is all of his need to know information."

I read what I've just been handed, and my eyes widen in shock. "Are you sure you don't want me to leave him to it? I'm sure he'd make a better manager than me, he's certainly got the experience." The question is asked before I can stop myself, and I instantly regret being so hasty when I see hurt flit across Bettie's face.

"No, I don't want Tomas Jenson running my resort, I want *you* to run it Samantha and don't you forget it, nor make me regret it young lady." She says sternly, but I see the affection in her eyes. "He's not your boss, and while I wouldn't call him your equal either, I think you'd do well to consider his ideas when they're offered. He is here to *help* you, not take over. Although, I have told him that he can manage the activities side of things. He's a bit of an adrenaline junkie, so I thought that giving him that to focus on would be for the best." I keep reading the information on him and realise that was probably the best thing to do with him.

"You're right, he's definitely got the qualifications to back him up in that area." I agree with Bettie wholeheartedly as I continue to read the list of activities he pursues. Including, skydiving, surfing, skiing, four wheel driving, scuba diving, wind surfing, fishing and more. So much more! "I'll be glad for the help in that area for sure."

"I'm glad you can see it for what I meant it to be. I'm sorry to just spring it on you, but I didn't want to say anything until I knew for certain he was going to take me up on my offer. He can be, how should I say it? He's very much a fly by the seat of his pants kind of guy, and I didn't know if this would be his kind of thing or not, but I've been looking for a long time for the right person and think Tomas is it. We need to bring some fresh blood and fresh activities into the resort, and he's just the person for it." I go to agree with her, but she holds her hand up in the air to stop me. "I know you are capable Samantha, but we really need new activities, and I love you dearly, but the running of the resort is more than enough for one person to take on. Which is why I never did it myself, and searched for someone else to do it for years."

"I love you too Bettie, and I what I was actually going to say before you stopped me, was I agree. This will be really good for the resort, and as long as he runs everything by me before jumping into things, we'll be perfectly fine."

"He is well aware that you are the boss Samantha, but that being said, he *is* the manager of activities, so you're going to need to work together. I really hope you two can make it work because he is the best by far that I met up with."

"So, you've met him, in person?"

"Yes, I have, a couple of times now and he's a wonderful man. Full of life and fun. I think he'll breathe some new life into the old place. Not that you won't, I know you have plans in the making as soon as I get out of your hair. All I ask is that you give him a chance, OK?"

"I promise to give Tomas Jenson the chance to prove his worth around here." I smile at my mentor and I know, that in that moment, I had every intention of trying to let Tomas prove himself, if only I knew what I was promised back then, I might have begged her to let *me* choose the activities manager myself.

"Good! I'm glad. He should be here on the first flight tomorrow morning, unfortunately he couldn't get here before Jerry and I left for the new house this afternoon."

"I'm sure he'll be upset that he didn't get to catch up with you Bettie, but I promise we'll take good care of him in your absence, and make him feel at home."

"Oh, I'm sure he won't miss seeing me once he sees your pretty self, but thank you for saying so." She laughs.

"Um, OK. Did you have one of the old bungalows cleaned out for him to stay in?" I ask, because I haven't noticed any extra movement around the staff bungalows, and I know there are still a couple of empty ones.

"No, he actually has somewhere else to stay close by, so he won't be living in the resort."

"Oh." There's nothing else to say really, it's his choice, but I wouldn't want to live anywhere else, even if the bungalows are a little run down and outdated.

"Yes, he's a rather stubborn fellow, but when I offered a bungalow to sweeten the deal, he declined and said he already had somewhere to stay. I would guess that's got something to do with how I managed to get him to agree to come work for you."

"No doubt." I say, wondering where the hell he's going to stay. It's not like there's a large choice of places that aren't resorts or hotels of some description. I shake my head to clear my thoughts, because it's none of my damned business where he chooses to lay his head once he leaves work for the day.

"OK, let's get to this surprise party, you guys are holding for me, I wouldn't want to be late." Bettie proclaims.

"There's no party." I start to protest, until she gives me the look. You know the one mothers give their kids every minute of the day. Roughly translated it means, 'don't bullshit me child'. I laugh loudly because there's no point in denying it, Bettie knows everything that goes on around here, so I shouldn't be surprised that she worked it out. "Alright, let's get going before we're too late and please, act surprised. The staff have put a lot of work into this for you. You're going to be missed around here Bettie."

"Stop it or you'll have me in tears before we get there." She whacks me lightly on the arm, then loops our arms and leads me towards the party she's not supposed to know about. I'm going to miss this woman like crazy. She's not just my boss and mentor, she's a mother figure and a close friend as well.

Chapter Two
TOMAS

Getting that phone call from Bettie Bryant out of nowhere was a shock, but a welcome one none the less. I gave her the impression that I had to think about her offer before accepting it, but the truth was, I didn't have to think too damned hard about it at all. What was there to think about?

Live on a tropical island – yes please!

Create adventure tours – yes please!

Get away from all the troubles surrounding me right – that's a hell fucking yes!

Live on a tropical freaking island! What kind of person would turn down an offer like that? Not me, I can tell you that. The only thing that I imagined could cause a problem was the new manager Bettie had put on so that she herself could retire.

Bettie and I had a met a couple of times, and I really liked her. When she first approached me about the position, it was the idea of working with Bettie that drew me to it, but she found the love of her life later on in life and decided to retire, handing the reins over to her second in command. Samantha Holt. I haven't met her yet, but Bettie showed me a picture of her so that I would know who she was when I got to the resort. All I can say is, maybe Bettie retiring wasn't such a bad thing after all.

I told Bettie that I wouldn't be able to get here in time for the surprise party that she wasn't supposed to know about, but I managed to get on an earlier flight. It's not until I walk into the resort that I realise I probably should have called first to let them know I was coming before just arriving on their doorstep, but I wanted to make it to say goodbye to the woman who quite possibly has changed my life.

I walk in the front doors, nodding to the guy at the front desk, and looking around, trying to decide where the party might be, when I notice the bar, and make my way towards it.

"I'm sorry sir, the bar is closed for a private function. Can I help you with something else?" I look back, and see the young guy behind the front counter starting to walk my way.

"Actually, you could, I'm looking for Bettie Bryant." As his mouth opens to answer me, I continue, "I'm guessing the private function is for her? Today is her last day on the premises, am I correct?" Crap, I hope I haven't gotten the wrong day.

He eyes me up and down, and that's when I notice his name tag, Jerome. Call me what you will, but this guy is *definitely* a *Jerome.*

"I can't give out that information, sir." Well, it's nice to know the staff won't share information without being expressly told they can.

"I'm sorry, I should have introduced myself, I'm Tomas Jenson." I say, holding my hand out for him to shake. Only he doesn't take my offered hand.

"It's nice to meet you Mr Jenson, but I still can't tell you that information."

Bettie didn't tell anyone I was coming? Damn it, did I come here on the promise of a job, only to be scammed? She was such a sweetheart, I can't believe she'd do this to me.

Jerome and I stand in the foyer looking at each other, both of us trying to decide how the hell this thing proceeds, when I hear a door open, then close behind me.

"Tomas, is that you?" I smile at Jerome and turn to speak to my new employer. "It *is* you! Why didn't you let me know you were coming in early? I would have had someone meet you. Jerome this is the new activities director, you weren't giving him a hard time now, were you?" she asks Jerome, and I get the feeling he enjoys being the gatekeeper around here, and only allows who he wants to behind the scenes.

"We were just introducing ourselves Ms Bryant, we didn't get further than names before you joined us." That's a very diplomatic way of putting what he was trying to do. He looks over Bettie's shoulder at me, quite obviously waiting for me to deny his claim, or challenge him. I have no desire to either.

"Jerome is quite right, we hadn't gotten any further than names *Bettie.*" I put a little emphasis on the fact that I'm using her first name, unlike some. "I was just asking Jerome where your party was being held, and being that he mentioned there was currently a private party in the bar, I thought that perhaps that's where you might be." My smile at Bettie is genuine, the one I send Jerome, not so much.

"Of course it is! Come, come. You should join us." She loops her arm through mine, and leads back to the doors she's just came out of. One hand on the door, poised to open it, she turns back to Jerome, a bright smile on her face, and says, "Everything is fine Jerome, Tomas is with me."

I can't help chuckling lightly at the stunned look on Jerome's face. As the guy on the front desk, I'm sure he's used to being able to do whatever he likes, especially with customers or random visitors, but I'm more than impressed to watch Bettie put him in his place, and she does it so pleasantly as well. That's quite the talent she has, one I wish I possessed myself if I'm being honest, I'm rarely that tactful.

"Are you sure there isn't something you needed? You did come out of the bar for a reason, or are you going to tell me you just sensed that I was here, and you wanted to check out the foyer to see if you were right?" I question her, half serious about that last part, as we head into the bar.

"What?" She asks me, looking at me like she's a slightly confused, but doting grandmother, rather than the astute and rather shrewd business woman I know her to be. "Oh, no I was going out there to check something, but it can wait until later. I want to introduce you to everyone, but I can't wait for you to meet Samantha. After all, you're going to be working closely together every day, you need to get to know one another."

I eye her suspiciously, but I doubt she could have cooked this up easily. I mean even I didn't know I was coming in an entire day early, but I have this niggling feeling in the back of my mind that the woman is up to *something* never the less.

While I've been wondering what she's up to, Bettie has walked us up to the bar, where a few people are gathered, laughing, and having a drink, but it's one beautiful woman with dark brown hair and bright green eyes that draws my attention, and I feel an instant attraction to her.

"Tomas Jenson, I'd like you to meet Samantha Holt. Samantha, this is Tomas, your new activities co-ordinator. I found him out in the foyer, aren't I lucky?"

"I thought you weren't supposed to be here until tomorrow." She asks, not unkindly per se, but before can answer, Bettie does it for me.

"Well, it would appear he managed to get an earlier flight. Aren't we lucky?" Betties asks, her eyes boring into Samantha's. If I had to guess, either Samantha isn't in favour of me being here, or this whole thing is a surprise to her. Honestly, I hope it's the latter, because I'm not sure if I can win her over if it's the first, and I *really* want to win this woman over. I've felt an instant attraction to women before, but never this pull to a woman before.

"It's nice to finally meet you Samantha, Bettie has told me so many great things about you." I say, holding my hand out for her take in hers. I really hope she takes my hand in hers.

"I'm glad one of us had heard of the other before this morning." She mumbles, but she takes my hand in hers, and I feel the jolt of her touch up to my shoulder. I think Samantha feels it too, because she looks a little startled, and takes a deep breath before speaking again. "It's nice to meet you too, Tomas. I'm looking forward to going through some of the ideas you've got to see if they'll fit in with our clientele." She smiles, and it's warm enough, but I am one hundred per cent certain that I was just on the receiving end of her polite customer service smile, and I hate it.

I don't want to say anything to Bettie in front of Samantha and the rest of the staff seeing as how I'm the new guy in town, but I thought I was getting to decide what I was and wasn't going to be offering as far as activities were concerned. Not complete free reign, but not too far off. I don't want to have to argue with someone else to get things done.

Before Bettie leaves today, we're going to have a talk about what I expected, and what she's told Samantha about my position. From the whispered snarky comment, and strained smile, I'm going to assume that Bettie hasn't been as forthcoming with her replacement, and protégé as she has with me.

Things could get interesting pretty quickly, *or* my time in Sandy Cove could be over before it's even begun.

"Come on Tomas, let me introduce you around to some of the staff and locals that have come out this afternoon."

"Of course Bettie, lead the way." I nod and smile at Samantha, and the couple of people standing with her, and then let Bettie lead me to a new group of people to meet.

I try to show an interest in every person she introduces me to, but I can't get those beautiful green eyes out of my head, and I can't shake the feeling I'm being watched, but every time I turn around to check, no-one is looking my way. I have my suspicions about whose eyes are on me, but I never catch her looking. Maybe she's not as unaffected by me as I first thought. This could make things very interesting.

Chapter Three
SAMANTHA

When I saw Bettie walk into the bar, her arm looped through the arm of the sexiest man I've ever seen, I swear my heart stutters for a few seconds, and I forget to breathe. When they reach our group, and Bettie introduces us, my heart stops for a completely different reason.

No matter how handsome, or attracted to this man I am, nothing can ever happen between us. I won't let it. I've seen the damage that follow relationships in the workplace. I have both first-hand knowledge, and been witness to the horrible fallout, and that's why my first rule is no workplace relationships, especially now that I'm the one in charge. Which is why I pulled the pin on the friends with benefits arrangement I had with Joey, the masseuse that works at the resort.

When I take Tomas' offered hand in mine in greeting, I feel an electrical current all the way up my arm, and I'm surprised. I've never felt that at just a touch with anyone else, ever. It takes everything in me, and my need to be professional, to not yank my hand out of his grip. Instead, I look him in the eyes, and that was a *huge* mistake. He's got these dark brown eyes, that remind me of melted chocolate. He smiles, and that's when I realise he's got tiny golden specks in those chocolate eyes of his, and they're glimmering with amusement right now.

"It's nice to meet you finally Samantha." He smiles, and I can see his lips moving as he continues to speak, but I'm still stuck on the timbre of his voice.

"It's nice to meet you too, Tomas. I'm looking forward to going through some of the ideas you've got to see if they'll fit in with our clientele." I smile sweetly at him, it's the same smile I give our visitors that can be hard to please. I see his smile dim a little, and I take it as a small victory. My guess is, Bettie told him he'd have full control over the activities he would be offering our visitors.

She has a way with words that woman, and I have no doubt she said what he wanted to hear about the position she was offering.

I also know she's told *me* very little about Tomas Jenson, and exactly what he plans do here.

I watch them as they walk away, and Bettie introduces him to the other people in the room. He seems comfortable with her, and with meeting new people. I guess he needs to be in his line of work, he meets new people every day.

"The new guy is hot." Geri, one of my co-workers announces loudly beside me. "Wouldn't you agree Samantha ?"

I turn to look at her, before saying, "Geri, you know the policy on co-workers dating." I'm trying to be stern, but kind.

"Pfft." She says with a wave of her hand. "Bettie never cared too much as long as we don't bring any drama into the resort."

"Well, Bettie is leaving today, and she put me in charge. I don't think workplace romances are appropriate or desirable, because you can't keep the emotional drama out of the resort when things go wrong."

"Who said things would go badly? I mean did you *look* at that man? He's the very definition of sexy, and I wouldn't mind checking him out, if you know what I mean?"

Geri has never been one of my favourite people, she's brash and rarely has a kind word, but her assessment of Tomas is really grating on my nerves.

"He's not a sex toy Geri, and I think you'd do well not to talk about people as if they were."

"I'm sure he wouldn't mind being used and abused like a sex toy. He looks like he'd quite enjoy it actually." She grins at me, knowing full well that she's pushing my buttons, and I'm hoping she thinks it just because I'm not a fan of workplace romances, and not the fact that my body is buzzing after just the touch of his hand.

"That's enough Geri." Suzi, her co-worker tells her, shaking her head. "You get carried away, and take things one step too far. Leave the man alone, he literally just got to the island, at least let him settle in before you try to jump his bones."

The thought of Geri jumping Tomas' bones makes me feel ill, but if that's what he wants, I can't, and won't stop him.

"Excuse me." I say, stepping away from Geri, and her group of friends that I'm not sure how I got involved in conversation with. Behind me I hear sniggers, and giggles, I have no doubt they're poking fun at me, and my rules. I'd like to say it doesn't hurt, but it does, not that I would ever let them see that. I learnt as a teenager not to show the 'mean girls' any weakness, and I'm not about to start now.

Instead, I float around the room, talking to the other staff that are coming in to say goodbye to Bettie, and then heading back to work again. I keep one eye on Tomas as well, even though for the most part, he's joined at the hip to Bettie. I'd be offended with her showering him with so much of her undivided attention, except that I know that she's making the effort to introduce him to everyone to make him feel comfortable being here. Not that I imagine the man ever feels like he doesn't belong wherever he is.

I get caught up in a conversation with Sylvie, a local who has been asking me if there are jobs available at the resort for a while now, about a new idea I have for one of the buildings on the grounds. We're deep in conversation, and I don't hear him walk up behind me until I feel the zap of his touching my lower back, and I feel my body tense at the warmth of his hand.

"Sorry Sylvie, I don't mean to interrupt your conversation, it was looking pretty intense, but I have to take Samantha away." I'm about to protest, when he sends a smirk my way, making me want to kiss it off his lips. "At Bettie's request, of course. She would like to talk to us alone for a few minutes."

"Why? I mean a meeting between us can wait surely? All these people are here to celebrate her retirement." Tomas doesn't answer me, he just shrugs his shoulder, and looks like he doesn't have a care in the world, it's as frustrating as hell.

"People are here for the party Samantha . Not saying we're not all going to miss Bettie, but it's not like you can or *would* say no to a meeting with Bettie." Sylvie laughs. Looking towards Tomas she says, "Bettie is a force to be reckoned with, and while I'm not saying that Samantha here won't be able to do the job just as well, if not better than Bettie, there will never be another Bettie. You should almost be grateful that you're coming in under Samantha ."

With a few innocent words, Sylvie has me picturing having Tomas under me, and coming. I feel the blush heat my cheeks, and I know he knows what I'm thinking, because he's looking me in the eyes, a lopsided smirk spreading across his lips, and I can't bring myself to look away.

"We should go." He speaks, jarring my brain back into working properly, and offering his arm for me to take, but I don't. I can't touch him right now.

"Right, yes. I'll catch up with you later Sylvie, we still have to set up a meeting to discuss that spa idea, so don't leave without talking to me today, OK?" Sylvie smiles and nods, looking at Tomas' offered and then rebuffed arm, and her smile gets wider.

"I'll be sure to see you before I leave Samantha ." I nod and head towards the door.

Chapter Four
TOMAS

The bar isn't as dark as I'm sure Samantha wishes it was right now, because I watch as a beautiful blush works its way from her neck up to her cheeks. I can't help the smile that curls my lips, because now I know she's thinking the same thing I am.

Samantha on top, riding my cock until we both come. Hard.

Now it's my turn to stumble over my own feet as we walk out of the bar to meet Bettie. I have no idea what she wants, but I wasn't going to tell her no. For one, it meant I got to go and talk to Samantha again, and for two, Bettie is still my boss.

"Are you OK there?" Samantha asks, as I make my feet work properly again.

"Fine." I say, smiling at her. She's probably wondering why Bettie hired a clumsy idiot as an adventure activities manager.

"If you're sure." She says without looking at me, and continues walking to Bettie's office, which I assume is now Samantha's office. Then I wonder where *my* office is.

"Samantha, Tomas. Come in, and close the door." Bettie insists. "Take a seat." She waves a hand at the chairs on our side of the desk she's sitting behind, and I can feel Samantha bristle beside me. I battle to hide a smirk, because I was right, this *is* her office now, and she's been relegated to a guest in it, just like me.

"Of course Bettie. What can we do for you? You're supposed to be enjoying your retirement party, not bringing the two of us in for a meeting." Samantha says through slightly gritted teeth, but with a smile. Making me believe it's actually *my* presence that she doesn't appreciate.

"Ohh I just wanted to get you two on the same page before I left, and people are more than happy to be left alone to party for a while." She tells us with a wave of her hand. "But you two, you two need my attention." She says while looking through a file on her desk.

I look over towards Samantha to get a read on what she's thinking, and even though I don't know her very well yet, part of my job is reading people to know how they're really feeling about any of the adventures I take them on, and experience tells me that she's none to impressed. When she doesn't look my way, I sigh and look back to Bettie, to see her still shuffling papers around.

I feel like I'm sitting in the principal's office waiting for my punishment or my parents to show up. Hopefully, my parents aren't here, because as much as I'd love to see them, I don't think right now would be the time for a mini family reunion. My Mum behaves like she hasn't seen me for years, even when in reality it could have been months, weeks, days, or even hours. She's like that with my siblings too, but I'm the crazy child who goes parachuting, hang gliding, rock climbing, and everything else in between.

"Sorry, I was looking for something, and ohhhh I found it!" Bettie's voice breaking the silence makes me jump a little.

"You're a little jumpy for an adventures manager aren't you?" Samantha whispers loudly, sarcasm dripping off her tongue.

"I was thinking about other things smart arse, and wasn't expecting Bettie to speak. It's pretty quiet in here you know."

"Well, she asked us in here so that she could speak to us together, why I don't know, so I assumed she'd be talking at some point." She speaks to me, but she keeps her eyes directed Bettie's way.

"Well, it's been quiet for a while, so I was thinking other thoughts. My apologies for not just sitting here like a statue waiting for someone to speak." And now it's my tongue dripping with sarcasm. This is not how I envisioned this meeting to go damn it!

"All right kids, that's enough." Now I feel like I've been reprimanded by my grandmother. "I was really hoping you two would get along but perhaps I was wrong. Maybe I should hang around for a few more weeks to make sure this transition runs smoothly, or to find another way to make something work if it doesn't."

"NO!" We both cry together. We finally found something we agree on!

"Bettie, you don't have to do that. We've worked hard together all these months so that you could retire and move to the other side of the island with

Patrick. Tomas and I can work together, we don't need you to stay around and wrangle us like we're toddlers. We're both adults, we can work it out." Bettie looks between the two of us, and you can see on her face that she just doesn't believe Samantha . Yes, I shortened her name, Samantha takes too long to say and too much brain power right now.

"Absolutely. You've got your plans, and we have ours. Samantha and I can work out any of the finer details between the two of us."

"*Tomas's* right." Samantha says, emphasizing the change in my name to match hers. "While I wish you'd given me a little more notice about his arrival, and your plans to hire him, now that he's here we can make it work." Damn, she makes me sound like an annoying prickle in her foot.

"I told you before we headed to the party I am sorry about the notice Samantha. I didn't do it on purpose, and I know you think I did young lady, but I didn't. When I found out Tomas was out of contract with his last adventure company, I jumped on the chance with the hope that he was looking for a change. A change of pace and scenery. He's the best in the business." Bettie looks from where she was daring Samantha to challenge her, over to me. "At the risk of sounding like a creepy old stalker lady, I knew who you were, and I've been following your career for a while now. I knew I wanted to offer adventure trips to our guests, but I also knew who I wanted to run them. Then Patrick came along, and well, retirement happened slightly earlier than I originally planned. Samantha was ready though, so I have no misgivings in that respect. None at all. She knows this resort, and this island inside out, back to front and upside. You couldn't have anyone better by your side to help you get your adventure tours up and running." I swear the absolute steel in her eye contact is making me feel like I'm actually being interrogated, not starting a new job that she's already given me.

"I'm flattered Bettie. A little scared but flattered that you took such a keen interest in my career." I smile at her, trying to charm her a little like I did when she came to me to offer me the job. It's not working, and I see Samantha smirk out of the corner of my eye. "I wouldn't say I'm the *best* in the business, but I'm definitely in the top five." I say, trying to sound slightly modest.

"You're being too modest, and you know it Tomas." Bettie snorts. "Well, with the pleasantries over, let's talk about what Tomas being here means for the resort, and you Samantha."

With that, we get down to business. The business of who is in charge of what, who answers to who, and who gets the final say on everything.

The simple answer is, Samantha Holt gets the final say.

If I don't agree, and we can't come to an agreement, then Bettie has to be called in, and Bettie does *not* want to be called in very often if at *all*.

We all agree, and Bettie makes us read a contract which states everything that we discussed, and then asks us to sign it.

Samantha hesitates for a few seconds, and I wait to see her move before I jump to sign on the dotted line. I want this job, in fact, I need it, but that doesn't mean I want to forfeit any control over it if I don't have to. Then, she sighs and signs her name, and I follow along right behind her.

What the hell. In for a penny, in for a pound right? I've got nothing to lose here if the tours don't work, so signing the contract works for me if it works for *Samantha.*

Chapter Five
SAMANTHA

My hesitation in signing the contract isn't the contract itself, because it's almost entirely in my favour. My hesitation comes from Bettie wanting Tomas to be the one who runs the tours. I don't know what it is about the man, but I'm not comfortable around him at *all*. The fact that a few female employees have already expressed how attractive he is, and how they'd like to 'date' him worries me. While the rule isn't written into any employment contracts, personal relationships between staff isn't exactly encouraged. It makes for uncomfortable situations when, and if the relationship sours, because generally speaking one person always ends up leaving the business.

Being that Bettie wrote a probation period into the contract for Tomas is a relief, and I know it's something she put in for my sake. I can feel Tomas watching me, waiting to see if I'm going to agree with the conditions, and sign the paperwork. I think part of my hesitation is to make him sweat a little. I don't think too many people tell him no, or make him accountable for his actions too often.

I hear him let out a breath I didn't realise he was holding when I sign on the dotted line, and follows suit a split second after me. When I look up from the paperwork, I find Bettie smiling from ear to ear. Before anyone can speak there's a knock on the door, then it opens without further invitation.

"Bettie, darling, people are wondering where you are, you're missing your own party!" Patrick says as he walks into the office. "Oh, sorry I didn't know you had company. Hi Samantha darling, how are you?" He walks over towards my chair, and I stand up to give him a hug. He kisses my cheek, squeezing me in a tight hug.

"I'm good Patrick, how are you? Are you looking forward to having Bettie to yourself after today?" I ask him. The smile he gives me as he pulls out of our embrace answers the question for me.

"I sure am sweetheart." He leans in close to my ear, and whispers loud enough for the others to hear him, "Between you and me, I don't think she's going to be able to keep her distance from the place. I think I've got my work cut out to keep her busy, and her thoughts away from here."

"Between you and me, I think you might be right." I agree with him, and we both laugh.

"That's enough out of you two." Bettie admonishes, but has a smile on her face, and a twinkle in her eyes.

Patrick steps away, turning his attention towards Tomas. "And this young man must be Tomas Jenson. It's nice to finally meet you young man, Bettie has told me good things about you." As Patrick moves towards Tomas to shake his hand, I look over at Bettie, and she meets my eyes with an unapologetic smile while shrugging her shoulders.

"It's nice to finally meet you Mr Bryant." Tomas the suck up says, as he takes Patrick's hand in his, and shakes it with a confidence that is sexy as hell.

"Patrick, call me Patrick Tomas, Mr Bryant was my father, and he's no longer here." Patrick looks my way with a smile. "We're all family here, aren't we Samantha? That means there's no formal titles used, we're all on a first name basis." There's mischief in Patrick's eye that I don't like, but before I can say anything, Bettie speaks.

"That's enough teasing Patrick, and that's enough business today, I just wanted to get that out of the way before we relaxed too much. I was going to be here tomorrow when you arrived Tomas, but now I don't have to be, because it's all done now." Bettie smiles broadly at us, gently pushing us all out the door, and locking it behind her. "Right now though, we've got a party to get back to." She loops her arm through Patrick's, hands over the key to the office, and leads the way back to the bar.

"Shall we?' Tomas asks from beside me, holding out his arm like the gentleman I'm assuming he's not, so even though he's being very charming, I brush past him to follow Bettie and Patrick. "So, that's a no then to my chivalrous offer?"

"I don't need any help getting back to the bar in the resort that I know better than the back of my hand, but thanks for the offer." I say, giving him a sweet as sugar smile when he catches up with me, and falls into step beside me.

"I didn't mean to suggest that you were anything except a capable, strong, independent woman Samantha, it was meant as a friendly offer, that's all." He assures me, and I can feel his gaze on the side of my face, but I don't look his way, I look ahead to where we're walking. When I don't say anything in reply, he places his hand gently on my elbow as I pull open the door to the bar, and I feel like the whole room quietens, and looks our way as we make our way over to the bar.

I seriously need a drink right now. We both order a drink, and then the chatter and general noise starts back up, I can finally relax a little.

"Vodka's a bit strong for a work function don't you think?" Tomas says from beside me, and I can't help but wonder what he'd say if I told him *he's* the reason I feel like I need the damned vodka. I won't tell him though, because I have a feeling that he'd be proud that he has any kind of effect on me. "I mean, you know what you can handle, but you're the boss now, you shouldn't get tipsy." He advises as he takes a swig of beer from the frosted glass in his hand.

I narrow my eyes, and say, "It's one drink *Mr Jenson*. I don't think it's going to hurt anyone, myself included, and employees need to know that the boss is human too and that she can relax. If you don't agree, that's your issue. Welcome to island life, we're a bit more relaxed here than in the big smoke." Without giving him a chance to respond, I walk away to find someone else to talk to. Someone who won't make feel like killing, hopefully.

I work my way around the room, nursing my *one* glass of vodka and soda, mingling, smiling laughing, and joking with employees, suppliers, and locals alike. The whole time I can feel his gaze on me, watching everything I do. I know I *should* be introducing him to people to make his transition into Sandy Cove easier, but I'm on such a delicate edge of emotions today that I can't deal with him as well.

Making my way back over to the bar, I place my empty glass on the bar as Tim the bartender comes over, and takes it away with a smile, bringing me back a bottle of water. I smile gratefully, glad that he knows me so well that he can read my damned mind.

"His gaze has followed you around this room for the past hour, you know that, right?" I jump slightly when Sylvie speaks beside me. I didn't realise anyone was that close to me, and I wish I'd taken more notice of my surroundings. I'm definitely more aware than that usually.

"Hmmm?" I don't look at her. "Who's doing what now?" I ask.

"You know exactly who's doing what Samantha . The room crackles with electricity when you two are in close proximity to each other. He wants you, and I think you want him too."

That grabs my attention, and before I can stop myself I look at her, and ask, "He does? Really?" I look up, because I can *feel* someone watching me. It's him. Tomas is standing on the other side of the room, talking to Lee and Mark, two guys that we've got on the books for boat charters and four wheel driving trips, but while Tomas is nodding and smiling at them, his focus is on me.

"Yes, he does Samantha ." Geri says with a laugh.

"It doesn't matter if he 'wants' me or not." I tell them, breaking eye contact with the man in question, and dragging my attention back to my friends. "It's never going to happen."

"Why can't it happen Sam? You're a gorgeous, funny, and loving human being, who deserves love and happiness." She leans in close, and lowers her voice so that only the two of us can hear her over the music and noise of people talking. "And you and I both know you were never going to find forever with Joey. He was a fun time, but he was never a long term plan."

"Joey and I, we were never together Geri." She snorts, and rolls her eyes at me.

"You can't bullshit me, Sam. I know it was never anything serious, for either of you really, but he was definitely more into you, and interested in taking it further than you ever were." She nods in the opposite direction to where Tomas is, and I look over to see Joey watching us. He raises his glass, and nods at us, smiling. I smile back, then turn my attention back to Geri.

"I'm his boss Geri, nothing good could come out of any kind of relationship between us."

"I'm not letting you know that I know about you two for any reason other than to let you know that happiness wasn't going to be found there. Not to mention, he never looked at you the way the new activities manager does."

"And how's that?" I ask before I can stop myself.

"Like he wants to eat you alive!" She moves a little closer again. "And I do mean *eat* you alive Sam. He looks like he would spend the time to make sure you were ready for every damned inch of him. You have to admit, he's a handsome man. Charming to boot."

"Sure, if you like those cocky, adrenaline junky types." I say with a little more bitterness than necessary, and I cringe the minute the words are out of my mouth.

"Ohh Samantha , sweetie, you've got it so bad for this guy." Sylvie laughs.

"No, Sylvie I don't. It doesn't matter, because we work together. I'm his boss."

"Where is he now?"

"He's talking to Patrick." I answer her question without hesitation, and it's not until I hear her laughter that I realise that I just proved her point for her. "It doesn't matter what kind of chemistry you think we have Sylvie, it's not going to happen."

"Sure it's not sweetie. You tell yourself whatever you need, to convince yourself of that." She says laughing. "Don't tell me I didn't warn you."

"There's nothing to warn me about."

"So, if I was to ask him out, you wouldn't object?" My gaze is locked on his position, when I register her question.

"No." I say looking her in the eye. "I don't have any hold on him. He can go out on a date with whoever he likes."

"What if that date is with Geri?" Sylvie asks with a knowing smirk, and I can't help the growl that escapes my lips. I just fucking growled over this guy, who the hell am I? "That's what I thought." She laughs louder.

"He can date whoever he wants, but I think he's got better taste than that." Don't get me wrong, Geri isn't a bad employee, I mean she does her job, and she does it well enough, but she chews up men, and then spits them right back out again.

"Sure he does boss lady, he likes *you*." She says with a wink, and I don't know what to say to that, so instead I look up to see where he is, because before Patrick stopped him, he looked like he was on his way here. He's still locked in what looks like a pretty serious talk with Patrick, which is funny because Patrick is normally pretty relaxed.

"I wonder what Patrick is talking to Tomas about. They both look pretty damned serious."

Geri looks up, finds where the two men are standing, and studies them for a minute or two. "I get the feeling that Patrick is warning the new guy off his favourite new resort manager."

"What?" I ask, turning sharply to look at her. "Why would you say that?"

"Come on Sam, everyone around here knows Patrick to be relaxed about everything except his wife, the resort, getting said wife to retire from said resort, and you. He thinks of you as the daughter they don't have, and he would protect you with his dying breath. I'm betting he's warning the new guy to keep it in his pants, and to not even think about it, because if he hurts you, they won't find his body."

I take in Sylvie's words, as I watch the two men talk. Suddenly they both look my way, catching me watching them. Patrick smiles, his face full of love, Tomas nods with a frown on his face. He says something to Patrick, who shakes his hand while a smile spreads across his face. I want to know what was said between them, but I don't want to ask Patrick, and I sure hell won't be asking Tomas any time soon.

All I know is that Patrick looks pleased with himself, and Tomas doesn't look as happy as he did a few minutes ago.

Chapter Six
TOMAS

I've been watching Samantha talking to her friends at the bar for a good twenty minutes or so. I had been talking to Lee and Max, two guys the resort has on call when guests want to go out on boat charters, or a trip to a local village, but my attention was only half on them. Most of my attention was taken up watching Samantha work the room.

I excuse myself from the guys, and start to make my way to the bar where Samantha is. I can tell that her, and her friend, Sylvie I think her name is, are talking about me, because every now and then, they look my way. Samantha is trying very hard to not notice I'm here, but it's not working out too well for her.

"Tomas, just the man I want to talk to." Patrick steps in front of me, stopping my progress to the bar, and Samantha.

"Patrick, what can I do for you?" I ask him, distracted by my desire to go talk to Samantha.

"You can look after her." He says. "By staying away from her."

"I'm sorry, what?" I ask, my gaze cutting away from watching Samantha, to look at the man standing in front of me.

"Samantha." He states simply.

"What about her?"

"I can see the way you look at her, the way you've been watching her since we got back to the party, and I can see that you're interested." I don't respond, I don't know this man, and his wife is my boss, sort of, I'm not going to say anything that risks me not being able to keep my job. "Can I offer some advice from an old man, to a young one?"

"Sure." I answer, not sure where this conversation is headed, or whether I actually want to hear what he has to say.

"Tread carefully. Make sure you want her for her, and that you want to have a real relationship with her. She's had some, let's say negative experiences in her past, which has caused her to concentrate on business. So, while I want to see her happy, if you're not planning on sticking around, I'm asking you not to start anything with her."

"Why wouldn't I stick around?" I ask him, confused as to why he thinks I wouldn't want to stay here on the island.

"You're an adventure, and adrenaline junkie. You rarely stay in one place for too long." He leans in closer so that only I can hear him. "And the three of us know why you needed this job in the first place, Tomas, so I think it would be best for all involved if you keep away from the woman we love like a daughter. Do I make myself clear?"

I told Bettie why I wanted the job when she first approached me. I was honest with her, and although I had the feeling at the time that she already knew my reasons for taking the job, but she never confirmed it. I guess I should have assumed that she would share that knowledge with her husband, but I didn't really think about how much influence he might have on her decisions with the resort. I know it's been her baby for a very long time, long before she met Patrick, so I guess I took it for granted that he wasn't involved in it. Maybe he's just concerned about Samantha, but either way, while I can't say I'm impressed with his not so subtle threat, I'm not going to start anything with the man about it. I don't see the point in creating an enemy, nor do I have any inclination to set him straight. "Crystal."

"Good lad, I'm glad we agree." He says, shaking my hand, then slapping me on the shoulder, and walking away to talk to someone else.

I look back over at the bar to where I last saw Samantha standing, only to realise she's no longer there. I quickly scan the room to see if I can spot her, and the disappointment of not finding her anywhere settles in me like a weight.

"You look like you just lost your dog." I look to my right, and Max is standing there. "Do you want another drink?" I hear a grunt to my left, and look over to see Lee standing there.

"Sure, why not." I tell them. It will be my last drink, because I have no intention of getting drunk at my very first work function, whether I'm officially an employee yet, or not, making friends with these two will help me find my feet with my new job.

"So, what did Patrick say to you? Was he laying down the law to you?" Max asks, staring into his empty glass, waiting for the bartender to bring him another beer.

"What do you mean?"

"Oh, just that he likes to throw his weight around like he's the boss sometimes." Max replies with a shrug, meeting Lee's eyes over my head. I look at Lee, and he gives me one sharp nod of agreement. The man doesn't say much, but he still manages to communicate.

"Does he have anything at all to do with the running of the resort?"

"Nah, Sandy Cove has been Bettie's baby since she was probably Samantha 's age. She bought it for a steal from the previous owners after they ran it into the ground. Rumour has it that Bettie's first husband died in some horrific accident, but he was loaded. He left everything to Bettie, and they hadn't started a family yet. She came here for a break a few months after he died, but when she got here the reality was a far sight different from the brochures, and pictures on the internet. Sandy Cove had certainly seen better days."

"Are you two gossiping again?" A female says from behind me, and both the guys body language changes instantly. They stiffen, and look like they've bitten into a lemon.

"Wouldn't want to take your hobby away from you Geri." Lee says, his voice little more than a growl of disgust.

She snorts out a laugh, and rests her hand on my bicep in a move that would be considered creepy if I did the same thing to her, but I don't want to offend her, so I don't shrug her off just yet. "Oh you know me boys, I'm just interested in knowing about my friends' lives." She flips her hair, and giggles like a school girl, and that's when I move far enough away from her that her hand slips out of my arm. I look at Max, and give him nod of thanks, because he moved back so that I had enough room to move.

"More like you like to know everything going on so that you can use it against your co-workers don't you mean?"

"Oh Max, darling, you're giving Tom here the wrong impression of me. He's new, and doesn't know you're joking around."

"No joking." I hear Lee mumble, and Geri throws a dirty look his way that would cut down a lesser man, but when she turns back to me, she's all smiles and innocence.

"Tomas."

"I'm sorry what?" She leans in a little closer like she can't hear me, and I lean back out of her way.

"My name. It's Tomas, not Tom. No-one calls me Tom." Never Tom.

"Well then, that can be my name, and my name only for you." Geezus, does this woman know how to turn down the flirting?

"No, it can't. I'm sorry Geri, but I won't answer to it. Never have, never will." I inform her with a smile, and hear Max snort next to me, and when I look around Geri, I see Lee smirking.

"Geri." I hear a woman's voice behind us say sharply, and Geri's body stiffens. "That's enough don't you think? You know the rules." The smile that crosses Geri's lips is kind of frightening as she turns to face the woman.

"What I know is, there are no rules against co-workers dating, Sylvie."

"You right, there isn't a specific rule, but you and I both know it's frowned upon. Now, why don't you leave Tomas to settle in and meet everyone. I'm sure Max and Lee would like to enjoy their drinks without you putting on a show for them."

"You Sylvie you're a real -."

"I wouldn't finish that sentence if were you Geri." I feel tingle race from the bottom of my spine up to the base of my skull when I realise who's standing behind me.

"Samantha , I didn't see you there." The smile on the woman's face becomes even weirder, and I can't describe it.

"No, of course not. You are still on Sandy Cove time, and you are still representing the resort, of which I am now the manager." Samantha says, her voice as cold as steel. I get the feeling there's no love lost between these two women.

"I think you should say your goodbyes to Bettie and Patrick, and then head home until your shift tomorrow." Sylvie advises her, and I see the fire light in Geri's eyes, and I'm waiting for the explosion, but she seems to think better of it.

"It was nice to meet you Tomas, I hope you can bring some fun, and excitement to the place." She comes closer to me, and before I can stop her, she leans in to kiss me, but I move my head just in time for her to miss my lips, and just get my cheek. "I'll see you soon."

"See you tomorrow Geri." Sylvie says, punching home that she wants the other woman gone.

"See you soon Tomas. I'll see you soon as well Lee and Max, of course." She blows them both a kiss, and walks off without looking back at the two women now standing with us.

"Not if I see you first, and manage to go the other way." Max says, and Lee mumbles his agreement with a vigorous shake of his head.

"I'm sorry about that, Geri can be a bit of a handful." Sylvie apologises.

"A bit! That's a *bit* of an understatement wouldn't you say? I mean that's like saying fire only burns a little bit when you touch it." Lee snorts out a laugh, and high fives Max.

"I'm not going to comment, except to say that I recommend you stay away from that one Tomas." Sylvie says with a warm smile.

"Thank you for rescuing me, I was trying to get away as politely as I could, but she didn't seem to be listening."

"Well, it didn't look like you were trying too hard, she *did* have her hands all over you, and you weren't moving." Samantha states, a hint of disgust and disappointment in her voice.

"You know how she can get Samantha , it definitely wasn't Tomas' fault if Geri had him in her sights, and you know that." Sylvie says, rolling her eyes.

"She sounds like a real treasure." I say to Sylvie, but my eyes are trained on Samantha. "I was just being polite, if there's a next time, I'll be sure to make her understand that I'm a no go. For her anyway."

"You can date whoever you like Mr Jenson, but I would rather you kept the females, or males if that's who you prefer, at the resort off limits."

"Is that a *hard*, and fast rule, Samantha?" I ask, using her first name on purpose, seeing as how she used my last name to purposefully put a distance between us.

"Technically it's not a rule, Mr Jenson, it just causes less drama this way." She grounds out, then reaches for Sylvie's hand and drags her away into the crowd.

"Wow, Tomas, you haven't even been here for twenty four hours, and you've already got it bad for Samantha and you've got Geri's gunning for you. We're going to have some fun with this guy around Lee."

I don't bother responding to him, his assessment isn't wrong. So, instead, I watch Samantha walk away, and work the room the entire time. She doesn't spare me another glance, and I don't see Geri again before I say my goodbyes to Bettie and Patrick. When Bettie asks me to stay, have some food and a few more drinks to get to know everyone a bit more now that it's just staff left, I beg off by telling her I'm tired from all the travelling today. I scan the room for what feels like the millionth time, but I can't find Samantha anywhere, so I leave for my new home without saying goodbye, and I feel like an arsehole doing it, but I need to find my bed so that I can get some sleep before I start my job tomorrow.

Chapter Seven
SAMANTHA

I know the minute Tomas leaves Bettie's party, and it's not because he says goodbye to me, oh no. Then again, I don't make any effort to speak to him when I realise what's going on either.

"Stop being a creepy stalker, and just go over there and speak to him Samantha ." Sylvie says beside me, making me jump, because I'd forgotten she was there. That's what the new *Adventures Specialist* does to me, and I've only known him for a few hours!

"He's already gone."

"I'm sure if you followed him, and called out his name to get his attention, he'd wait for you to catch up." She says, bumping her shoulder to mine, and winking at me when I drag my eyes from the door he just left through, to meet hers.

"He looked like he was in a hurry, and I'm sure he's got a lot of things to do to settle into his new place before he starts work tomorrow." I say unconvincingly. My body is trying to leave, to follow him out the damned door, but my brain stops me from moving.

"I'm sure you could help him adjust to island life Samantha ." She bumps my shoulder with hers again.

"I'm sure he's already got help lined up, Sylvie. He doesn't need my help for anything."

"I'm going to go out on a limb and say he wouldn't refuse your help. With *anything,* if you know what I mean?" She sends another wink my way, but before I can reply, a hand touches my arm, and a deep voice speaks beside me, making me smile.

"You know what Sylvie? I think Samantha is right this time, as she is most of the time." Patrick smiles at me. "I think she'd be smart to stay away from that one."

"Why do you say that Patrick?" I ask, curious as to his reasoning.

"Well, he loves to travel, he rarely stays in the same place for long, he's an adrenaline junky, and he likes the chase. The chase of the next high, which I have no doubt translates into his woman as well. You're not that kind of girl Samantha. You're sweet, kind and a homebody. You love it here, and I can't see you wanting to leave to follow him around the world while he catches his next fix."

"Even adrenaline junkies eventually settle down Patrick." Sylvie says, her voice full of annoyance. "I think Samantha is old enough, *and* smart enough to make her own choices about what and *who* she wants in her life."

"She sure does Sylvie, and that's what I meant. I don't think she needs *either one of us* trying to influence her decisions. Do you?" He narrows his eyes at my friend, but she doesn't back down, which is making me feel a little awkward.

"I know you *both* have my best interests at heart, but honestly, I'm concentrating on the resort for now. No man, Tomas or any other, is on my radar right now, so neither of you have to worry about me at all."

"What are you three looking so serious about? It's supposed to be a party you know?" Bettie says.

"Nothing darling." Patrick says, kissing her on the cheek, making me wonder why he wouldn't just tell her the truth.

"Ohh Samantha, don't you think that Tomas will be a great fit around here? He's not too hard on the eyes either is he? I mean, I know I kind of surprised you with him, but I think you two will get a long fabulously, if you get what I mean?" She says with a wink. Why is everyone winking at me today? "He's certainly nice to look at, and I saw the way he was watching you my dear, I think he's found something he likes here, and it's not just the job either."

"Now Bettie, darling, you leave Samantha alone. I'm sure she's more than capable of finding a man, or woman for that matter, all on her own. She doesn't need you matchmaking for her, and she just met this Tomas fellow, as did we, we know nothing about him."

"That's not true Patrick, and you know it! I think that Samantha, and Tomas would make an adorable couple, don't you think so Sylvie?"

"I do, yes." Sylvie agrees with a huge smile on her face.

"I think that Tomas would give her a little bit of spark, and Samantha would give him an anchor, something I think that boy desperately needs, even if he doesn't quite know that yet."

"Leave them be darling." Patrick says, grumpily.

"Fine." Bettie laughs, either not noticing the tension in the air, or simply not caring about it. "Anyway, what I came looking for you for was because we're going to get going. I'm tired, and I can't wait to get home. You have full control of the resort now Samantha, and I know, without a doubt in my mind, that you're going to be brilliant. Always remember, I'm just a phone call away if you need anything."

"That's it?" I ask, surprised.

"Yes, we've slowly gone around saying goodbye. I left you for last, because, well I'm going to miss you the most sweetheart, but I know you've got this." She moves in to wrap her arms around me, holding me in a tight hug for quite a few minutes.

"I need to breathe Bettie." I wheeze out jokingly, because I'm on the verge of tears, so I'd rather joke. She steps back, and Patrick takes her into his arms, holding her close as she sniffles into his chest.

"Come on darling, let's get out of here before the waterworks get out of control." He laughs, but I know that he doesn't want to see either of us crying. He waves to both of us, and then they're quietly slipping out a side door that leads out onto the beach. We usually have the doors open, but it's unusually chilly out there tonight.

We watch them disappear, and I turn to Sylvie. "I'm going to get out of here too. It's been a long day with plenty of curveballs that I didn't see coming, and I can hear my comfy bed calling my name."

"Are you sure?"

"Yes. Tell everyone to stay for as long as they want, but remember some of them still have work tomorrow, and I won't be accepting any call ins for hangovers." I laugh, as she squeezes me tight.

"You got it boss." She assures me with one more tight squeeze. "Now, go on home, and get some rest."

"Thanks Sylvie." I give her arm one more squeeze, and then make my way out of the bar. I get stopped by a few people along way, congratulating me on taking over the running of the resort from Bettie.

When I finally get outside, I take a deep breath, and decide to go for a walk along the beach before heading home. Walking along my favourite stretch of beach just out of sight of the main building of the resort, I pause for a few seconds, taking in another deep breath, and I let out a long, loud sigh. I spot my favourite rickety, old jetty, and make my way over to sit on it.

"That was a pretty big sigh, sounds like you might have a few things on your mind there Samantha." I jump, startled by his deep, but quiet voice.

"Holy shit Tomas, you scared the crap out of me!"

"Sorry about that, I didn't mean to, but you kind of just walked right by me, and I didn't want you to think I was stalking you or something when you finally realised I was here."

"I thought you were headed home?"

"I was, but then I decided to come sit out here, and enjoy the ocean for a little while. Guess that turned into a long while. I'm sorry for scaring you, I wasn't expecting anyone else to come out here."

"Well, I wasn't expecting anyone to be here at all. The staff are all still at the bar, and guests very rarely venture out this way, which is why I like coming out here." I don't know why I told him that. I also don't realise we've been walking and talking until my feet land on the worn wood of the jetty.

"Do you come out here often?"

"That sounds like some weird version of a really poor pickup line Tomas." I laugh. "I gave you more credit than that."

"You thought about my pickup lines?" Curiosity in his voice.

"Not really if I'm being honest, but I didn't think you'd go for corny. I thought you'd be more creative than that." I say, laughing again, as I sit down on the edge of the jetty, my feet dangling just above the water. I feel rather than see Tomas join me, as I look straight ahead out at the ocean.

"So, what I'm hearing here is, that you thought about what my pickup lines might be, and you had higher expectations from me than, *do you come here often?*" He says, and I can hear the smile in his voice, but I don't look at him, I continue to stare ahead when I answer him.

"I did expect more than the corny standard line, yes, but maybe I was giving you more credit than you deserved."

"I'm still stuck on the fact that you thought about what kind of line I'd use to pick you up." I can feel him looking at me when he talks, but I still don't look at his handsome face, because I'm afraid of what I might agree to if I do. "Samantha." He says, quietly in the stillness.

"Tomas." I say just as quietly.

"I really want to kiss you." It's a simple statement, right to the point, and I really appreciate it.

"I know."

"If I kiss you, will you let me, or will you hit me?" He asks me sincerely, and I hate that I've given him the impression that I would hit him or refuse his kiss. Then again, I don't want to want his kiss. I don't want to complicate my life, or his.

"Guess you'll have to find out." I answer, my voice barely above a whisper.

"Is that permission?"

I finally take my eyes off the ocean, and meet his hot gaze. His eyes flick between mine for about five seconds, and he must find what he was looking for, because he doesn't waste another second. His lips are on my mine before I can think about his swift movement. They're gentle, soft, and nothing like what I expected. Then his hand is twisted through my hair, and cradling my head gently in his hand to keep me just where he wants me. I moan, and he takes full advantage of it, pushing his tongue into my mouth to touch mine.

The man can kiss, I'll give him that.

Chapter Eight
TOMAS

My first mistake was not going straight home when I left the party. My second was spotting Samantha and not walking in the opposite direction when I realised who she was, but I will never regret kissing her. The feel of her lips on mine, and her taste will linger in my brain for ever, no matter where we go from here.

"We shouldn't." Samantha whispers against my lips, as we break apart just far enough so that we can catch our breath.

"Why not?"

"We just met for one."

"That was hours ago."

"What if someone sees us?" She asks, not making an effort to move away from me.

"I can leave." I loosen my grip in her hair, and on her hip.

"No!" She swallows hard, and closes her eyes, taking a deep breath. Even from this close, I can see the warring emotions moving across her face, as I pull further away from her. I'm not going to force myself on her, or anyone else, I've never had to before, and I never will.

"That's OK, I understand." Before I can step too far away, her hands that were resting lightly on my shoulders suddenly grip onto my biceps.

"You don't, you really don't." She lets out another quiet sigh. "Look, it's honestly not you, it's me."

"Got it." I try to step away from her, but she holds on tighter.

"I don't think you have, Tomas. I don't want to make a mistake. I've just taken over from Bettie, and I don't want the staff to think I'm not taking the position seriously."

"And kissing me tonight means you're not taking the job seriously? How does that work Samantha?" I can't help asking, because I'm fucking confused by her logic.

"It's not written in any of the manuals or contracts, and it's not especially frowned upon, but we don't recommend personal relationships between staff members, because I got burned by one in a previous position. I had to leave a really good job because I was made out to be a whore looking for the fast track to success. When I tried to explain what actually happened, and stood up for myself, let me tell you that I wasn't the one with the happy ending, he most certainly was. So, when I found out that Bettie was going to make me the manager here at Sandy Cove, I ended something that I had going on so that I could concentrate on the job."

"So you're not seeing anyone right now?" I want to make sure I haven't over stepped my boundaries, but I'm hoping that she wouldn't have kissed *me* if she was seeing someone else.

"No." She laughs. "Is that all you got out of what I just said? And shouldn't you have asked that *before* you kissed me?"

"I gave you the chance to say no Samantha." A frown taking over my face. "And all I heard in what you just said were excuses for not taking a chance."

"So, where do we go from here?" She asks, stepping closer to me.

"To be honest, I don't know Samantha." I reply, shaking my head slightly. "Are you telling me you don't feel this pull between us? This electricity, this spark? Because if you don't, I'll walk away right now, and we can be the co-workers it seems that you want us to be, but if you feel this." I can't complete my thought, because she pulls me impossibly closer, and plants her lips on mine in the hottest kiss I think I've ever been given.

"Tomas." She mumbles against my lips. "I feel it too, and it scares the crap out of me."

"I won't bite Samantha, not unless you ask me." I say with a grin, and she giggles, which is what I was hoping for. "We don't have to do anything, not tonight, not ever, if you don't want to. I would never pressure you into anything, sweetheart." I tell her, running my thumb along her jawline, and praying that she doesn't leave me standing on the ramshackle of a jetty we're standing on.

"I don't want to stop." She whispers. I can feel her uncertainty rolling off her in waves, and I don't want her to regret whatever happens tonight, tomorrow.

"Are you sure?" She nods her answer, but she can't look me in the eye.

"I need your words sweetheart."

"Pick up your bag."

"What? Why?"

"Pick up your bag and follow me." She repeats, a pleading in her voice and her eyes that I can't resist. So, I do as I'm told. I walk the few steps to where I left my bag, and pick it up. When I turn back to face her, she's already holding out her hand. I take it in mine, and she weaves our fingers together. With a shy smile she turns away from me, and leads me away from the jetty.

"Where are we going?" I ask.

"There's an old bungalow nearby that was fixed up recently, I thought we could go there. For some privacy." She answers me with a shy smile that I can't resist.

"Lead the way sweetheart." I say, squeezing her hand lightly.

She turns from me to lead the way, but not before grinning broadly at me, and it warms my dead heart. I'm still wondering why she's the one that's made me feel alive for the first time in years, when she stops walking.

"We're here." She's still talking quietly, and I can't help but wonder if it's because she doesn't want anyone to hear her, or if she's nervous. I don't get the chance to ask, because she opens the door to the hut, leading me inside without speaking. Closing the door behind us with my foot, I see her flinch when it's louder than either of us expected.

"Are there other huts that are close by?" I ask, curious as to whether we have neighbours that might have possibly heard that.

"No, not really." She blushes at her confession. That's when it hits me, she knows this resort like the back of her hand, and she knew this bungalow was away from the rest of them. She came here on purpose.

"So, we're all on our own here?" I ask. "You trust me enough for that, sweetheart?"

"Yes."

"Yes? To which part?" I ask, as she walks backwards, my hand still in hers.

"Both." She says with a wicked grin. "We're on our own here, *and* I trust you enough to *be* alone with you. Bettie wouldn't have brought you on board if she thought for even a second you were a crazed lunatic."

"Please don't talk about Bettie while you lead me to a bed, sweetheart." I smile at her.

"What do you mean?" She asks, a picture of innocence on her face. "You don't want to think about Bettie while we're, hang on what are we doing?"

The back of her legs hit the edge of the bed, making her giggle as she falls back onto the bed, pulling me with her. I land on top of her, and her laughter dies when our eyes connect.

I lean down and kiss her. It's gentle, almost sweet at first. Until I bite her bottom lip gently, then run my tongue over it to soothe the pain, and she gasps, giving me access to her mouth. Her hands roam up and down my back, over my shoulders, then back down again, and I can't get enough of her touch. Then her hands lift my shirt, and skim across my bare skin, and when I jump she moves as if she's going to stop.

"Don't stop. Your touch is amazing." I mumble against her lips, and after a second of hesitation her hands are back on my skin, making me shiver. Her touch is electric.

"Take your shirt off." She says, breaking our kiss *just* enough so that she can speak.

"Whatever you want sweetheart." Leaning up on one arm, only breaking contact with her lips long enough for the other hand to pull my shirt up over my head, and I toss it to the floor.

"I want you, Tomas." She says, looking me in the eyes, showing no hesitation.

"Are you sure Samantha?" I ask, looking in her eyes to see if she has any doubts at all. "Because we don't have to go any further if you don't want to."

"You don't want to?" A hurt look crosses her face, but it's gone so quickly I'm not sure if it was my imagination or not. Then she starts to push up on my chest, trying to get away.

"I want this Samantha. I want *you*, don't ever doubt that sweetheart." Her body relaxes under me, and she smiles up at me.

"Then you can have me, Tomas." That's all the permission I need, and suddenly we're left only in our underwear. Samantha in a matching bra and knickers, and me in my boxer briefs. "Do you have a condom?" She whispers into my neck as she licks, and kisses her way down to my collarbone, making it hard for me to think of anything else.

"Yes." It's all I can manage to say in answer to her questions, and she laughs.

"Well, you should get it, don't you think?"

"What? Right, of course. Don't move."

I'm off the bed, and fumbling through the pockets in my jeans before she can change her mind. I turn to look at her, hand with the foil packet held up in the air like I just won first prize in a weird competition.

"Come here." She says, curling her finger at me a few times. I'm back on the bed in half a heartbeat, making her laugh again. Never before have I enjoyed listening to a woman laugh at me when we're both naked, but I love listening to her laughter.

Ripping open the foil, she flings the empty wrapper away, then her hands are on my already too hard cock as she rolls the condom on me. My cock jumps at her touch, and with the anticipation of being inside her.

"Samantha." Her name comes out in a rasp that I've never heard in my voice before. If just her touch does this to me, how the hell am I going to manage to not blow my load too soon, and disappoint her.

"You won't disappoint me Tomas." She smiles at me, and I realise I must have spoken out loud by mistake. "I need you inside me Tomas, please."

"Are you sure? This is your last chance to say no Samantha, because I don't think I can stop once I'm inside you." I tell her, rubbing the head of my cock along the slit of her pussy, teasing her.

"Tomas, please." She pleads, while pushing her hips up to meet mine, and that's all the invitation I need. I run my finger through her pussy to see if she's ready for me, and she's so wet for me that I groan.

I try to go slow, inching into her pussy to give her the chance to adjust to my presence, but she wraps her legs around my waist, pulling me down, as she pushes her hips up to meet mine, making us both groan loudly at the sensation of me bottoming out in her.

"Fuck!" I spit out through clenched teeth.

"Exactly the point." Samantha explains, even as she's trying to catch her breath from the sensation of being full. "Move Tomas, now!" She demands.

Who am I to deny her, so that's exactly what I do. I pull out, and push back in time, and time again, until I feel her pussy starting to clench around me.

"I'm not going to last much longer sweetheart, you're gonna need to come for me. Now!"

"I – I'm." She stutters, pulling in a couple of large gasps of breath. "I'm going to. Oh Tomas! Oh God!"

"That's it sweet-." I don't finish the rest of the words because her pussy clenches hard around my cock and we're both coming. I rest my forehead on hers as we both catch our breath.

I take care of the condom, and then pull her into me for a full body hug. I wrap her up in my arms and my leg rests over her hip.

"Tomas." She starts, but I don't let her finish as I pull the covers up over us.

"Sleep now sweetheart. Sleep now." She rests her head on my shoulder, and I feel her body relax, and I let myself fall asleep as well.

Chapter Nine
SAMANTHA

I wake up with a smile on my face, and the sun warming it. I open my eyes with a start, because I'm wondering why the sun is on my face. I left the curtains open that's why! I move to close them, only to realise I can't move because there's an arm wrapped tight around my waist, with a hand holding my boob in it.

"What the fuck!?" Who the fuck is big spooning me, and why the hell is he naked? *Why* the hell are we *both* naked? The only thing I know for sure, is that my sleeping buddy isn't Joey, because even though I never let him stay overnight, he *did* insist on cuddling afterwards. That's when it all comes rushing back to me.

Tomas Jenson, the new activities specialist!

"Mmmm just give me a couple of minutes to wake up Samantha." Tomas mumbles into my shoulder, tightening his hold around my waist, and I freeze in place. I look around the room trying to get my bearings, and that's when I realise this isn't my house, so where the hell am I? "What's wrong sweetheart?" Tomas asks as he rests his chin on my arm, and looks over the side of my body to look me in the eyes.

"Nothing." I say, swallowing a large gulp of air, and giving myself a coughing fit.

"Take it easy beautiful, I don't want you to choke on air." He says while rubbing my back in gentle circles, and I just can't take it. I pull out of his embrace, pushing hard until he relents, and lets me out of the bed. "Are you sure everything is OK? You seem a little off this morning." He scrubs a hand over his handsome face, and continues. "What time is it by the way? I don't want to be late on my first day." He's smirking, and joking around, but it jars me back to reality.

"We can't be here. I can't be here. You should go, but wait until I'm gone. We can't leave here together." I ramble, the words all jumbled together as if they're really one word.

"What? Why can't we leave together?"

"Because then people will know."

"People will know what, Samantha?" The tone in his voice has changed from sleepy confusion, to disappointment, and anger has taken on his handsome features.

"They'll know what we did, Tomas."

"And what was that *Samantha?*" His voice now starting to reflect the anger on his face. "Are you embarrassed or ashamed about being with me, is that it?"

"No, that's not what I mean, and you know it." I reply, sighing in frustration. "You know why this can't work, why this can't get out. I explained all of that, didn't I?"

He sits up in the bed, the sheets falling down to the tops of his hips, revealing way more of his body than I need to see, because it's a magnificent body, and I love looking at it. My eyes rake up and down his body, taking all of him in, because this could be my last chance to do it, obviously.

"My eyes are up here sweetheart." His lips are smiling, but his face is screaming that he's mad.

"Sorry." I mumble, as his eyes take their time to look *me* up, and down. That's when I realise that I'm standing in the middle of the room stark fucking naked in front of this man. As I attempt to cover myself up with just my hands, his loud, deep laughter fills the room.

"Bit late for modesty don't you think, sweetheart?" An amused smile spreads across his face.

"It's never too late Mr Jenson!" I tell him, trying to maintain some dignity while standing in front of him naked as the day I was born.

"Oh we're back to Mr Jenson now are we, Ms Holt?" His low chuckle shouldn't send heat through my veins, but it does, and that scares the absolute crap out of me! "Don't you think that we could lose the formality after last night? I mean, we've seen each other naked. I've been inside you, Sam."

"Samantha." I remind him without thinking. "My friends call me Samantha."

"And now I call you Sam." I want to smack the sexy smirk right off his face, mainly because it sets my body on fire, and makes me want to press my legs together. I don't, because I'm not going to give him the satisfaction of seeing how he affects my body. Even if he already witnessed it last night.

"No, you don't. No-one calls me Sam."

"I do." He says stubbornly as he swings his legs over the side of the bed, getting ready to stand up. I start to protest, but he turns to face me, stretches the sleep out of his delicious body, and I lose the ability to speak. My god, who would have thought that all that outdoor activity would leave him with a body like *that*? Not me, I can assure you. "Are you OK, Sam?" he asks, taking a few steps towards me, and I hold up my hand to stop him, but he keeps coming.

"Stop." I demand, closing my eyes so that my brain can function. "Don't come any closer please Tomas."

"So, I'm back to Tomas am I? I wonder if I can get you to call me Tom? Do you think that might happen one day? Perhaps I can get you so ready for me, so horny, that I can convince you to call me Tom in that beautifully breathy voice when you're right on the edge of coming."

My eyes snap open, my retort right on the tip of my tongue. That is until I feel his bare chest touch my still out stretched hand, and once again lose my ability to think, or pull my hand away. The feel of the hard ridges of his chest under my hand is something else. I'm not an inexperienced virgin, I've had my eyes, and hands on more than one guy in my time, but Tomas is something else. Not even Joey who has the muscle tone that most guys want, ever made me feel like this with just a touch. It's not even a sexual touch, he's just really close!

"Wh-what are you doing?" I stutter.

"Well, I was going to the bathroom, but then you closed your eyes, so I thought I'd stop here to make sure you're OK. Are you?"

"Am I what?" I ask, confused.

"OK. Are you OK, Sam?" The simple answer? No I am fucking not, but I'm not going to tell him that, am I?

"No, I'm not." Apparently I am going to tell him that. What the hell is wrong with me? He's not the first guy I've ever seen naked.

"What's wrong? Can I help?" He asks while running his hands up, and down my upper arms. His warm, calloused hands that I shouldn't be enjoying, but I am. Still! I've never had this primal reaction to a man before.

"I need to get out of here." I pull out of his tender hold, I don't want his affection. "Shit! What time is it?"

"It's six o'clock." He sounds defeated but I can worry about his feelings right now.

"How do you now that?"

"Because I checked my phone before I got up from the bed, Sam." His phone? I don't even know where the hell mine is. It has to be in my handbag somewhere in here. "I left it on the bedside drawers last night before we undressed." I nod my head, agreeing without really understanding the logistics of his movements.

"I need to go home."

"This isn't your bungalow?" He asks, a frown on his when I look up from my search for my underwear.

"No, it's an old bungalow that was recently renovated. All of the bungalows in this area are original to the resort, and all of them need repairs, and fixing." I look up at him when I find my bra, and underwear. "In fact, this one Bettie was in a hurry to complete for the new activities specialist." He has the good grace to look embarrassed.

"I didn't know Bettie was doing that. This." He was looking around the room, taking it all in. "It looks amazing."

"Well, now you know." While he's talking, I pull my clothes back on, and look around for my handbag.

"You seem have an advantage over me now, Sam." He chuckles.

"What are you talking about now?" I ask, not looking up from my search.

"Well, it would seem that you have me at a disadvantage Ms Holt being that I'm completely naked, and you're now completely dressed again. What would Bettie say if she was to walk in here right now? I mean I'd like to keep my virtue intact on my first day in the new job, if that's OK with you?" He says it with a serious face, but there a mischievous smile on his face, and he confuses me. Who am I kidding, he's done nothing but confuse the hell out of me since I met him yesterday.

"Virtue." I snort, because he's joking. Right? "Says the man who slept with someone he hasn't even know for twenty four hours." His hands go to his hips, and his mouth hangs open in shock.

"Well, it takes two to tango Ms Holt, and I'll have you know, I don't always put out on a first date."

"We didn't even go on a date Tomas." I say, my frustration getting the better of me. "I'm leaving now to go to my bungalow, to shower last night off me, and to forget it ever happened."

"Now, I'm just insulted Sam. I mean that's just rude! I'm standing right here, and you're telling me to my face that I'm a mistake, something you regret." I can't help it, another snort escapes me, only this time it's not of laughter.

"Would you prefer I wasn't honest with you, Tomas? That I just left here after building up your ego, but then forging ahead every day as colleagues? Because let me tell you mister, the *only* thing we're going to be after I leave here, is the manager of Sandy Cove Resort, and the activities manager. Nothing more, nothing less."

"So, that's where we stand is it? We're nothing to each other?" He asks, and I can see the anger on his face. Good, he should be angry.

"That's exactly where we stand Mr Jenson. Whatever this was will *never* happen again, and we'll be co-workers, actually I'm your boss. That means this stays between us."

I don't give him a chance to argue with me, or to find out if he agrees with me, and will keep last night to himself. At this point, all I want is to get out of here, and back to my place. I can't think straight while I'm around him, and when he's naked, well my brain is completely fried.

"Bye Sam, see you at the office." He calls out as I swing the door open, and leave.

"It's Samantha to you." I say, leaving him standing in all his glory in the middle of the bungalow, and I don't look back. I won't be tempted to go back for round two if I can't see him naked anymore.

Chapter Ten
TOMAS

When I woke up, and Sam was still in my arms, I was surprised. Happy, but pretty surprised. I thought she might try to escape sooner, but I also assumed that this was her bungalow, which made me think that I was the one who would be kicked out this morning. Therefore, being left, naked, and standing in the middle of the room, was a shock to the system. Only topped by her informing me that Bettie had this particular one renovated for me. I wasn't expecting that.

When Bettie and I last spoke, she mentioned living here in the resort, and I told her I'd already arranged for somewhere to stay. She was surprised, because she thought that I didn't know anyone here, and she's not wrong. I'm not sure why I told her that I had somewhere to stay, except that at the time I thought staying in the same place I would be working would be stifling, especially given the fact that I don't have anywhere else to stay. Now that I know that she'd already gone out of her way to get this bungalow ready for me, I feel like an even bigger arsehole.

I make the decision on the spot that I'm going to go into the office, and speak to Sam. Maybe I can tell her that where I was going to stay fell through, and I'd like to use this space instead. If that was OK with her, and Bettie.

Decision made, I hop in the shower to make myself presentable, and then put on some fresh clothes from my duffle. I smile as I leave the bungalow, locking it behind me with the key Sam left behind. One of the things I've learned with my job is making a decision quickly, and sticking with it. Most of the time, it's a life and death kind of situation, and I need to think on my feet, it's put me in good stead for the situation I currently find myself in.

When I step into the office, the first thing I hear is Sam's voice, and it makes me smile. I know she's resistant to whatever this is that's going on between us, and I wouldn't think to tell her, her worries aren't warranted, *but* if she thinks we're going back to being nothing more than co-workers after last night, she's got another thing coming. And then coming again, just like she did last night. I smile again at my joke.

"No Geri, the dating policy at Sandy Cove hasn't changed." I can hear the frustration, and annoyance in her voice. I may have known her for less than twenty four hours, but I can tell when she's pissed. Believe me.

"Then why did I see you walking up from the beach to your place early this morning, looking dishevelled, and still in the same clothes you had on last night? Where were you?" Geri demands.

"I went for a walk down to the beach first thing this morning Geri, I didn't realise that was a crime, or that I answered to *you*. The last time I checked, I was the boss around here, not you." As I rounded the corner, I could almost see steam coming out of Sam's ears. The gall of this Geri woman to be calling her boss' actions out, no matter how new the position was.

"Isn't that down near where the new *adventure specialist's* place is? The one that Bettie busted our arses to get set up for him before he arrived?"

"Good morning Geri, Samantha." I nod her way, not really acknowledging her, and making a point to use her full name. "My new home is down near the beach. It's got a beautiful view, it was an absolute delight to wake up to it this morning, I hope for many more to come." Out of the side of my eye I see Sam flinch slightly, and a light blush crawl over her cheeks. Thankfully, Geri's focussed her attention on me, instead of her boss now.

"So, you watched the sunrise this morning did you?" Geri asks while running a hand down my arm, and I struggle not to flinch away from her touch. Letting her know that her touch bothers me won't help get her off Sam's back about us.

"No, I was too tired from all the travelling I did yesterday to get up that early, but I did see Ms Holt walking by my window when I managed to get up this morning." I tell her, my customer service smile plastered on my face. She doesn't know me well enough yet to know that she's getting the me that I give people I can't stand.

"So, she wasn't with you? You know, last night?" She asks in what I think she means to be a sexy purr, but sounds like a cat choking on catnip.

"Well now, I didn't say that." I tell her, as I gently remove her hand from my arm, and drop it by her side. I hear Sam's sudden intake of breath, and I know she's about to say something in her defence, so I rush on. "She did after all have to show me to the bungalow, and hand me the key."

Geri giggles, yeah that's not an attractive thing from a grown woman, especially when you can tell she's putting it on. "Oh I'm sure a big, strong handsome guy like yourself would have been more than capable of finding the bungalow on your own, but if you needed any help, you could have asked me." She tried to purr again, and it's just strange, as she attempts to paw at my chest this time. I grab her wrist, stopping her from touching me, and gently drop her hand back down by her side.

"I didn't need your help, I had Samantha to show me how everything works, and that was all I needed." I smile pleasantly at her. "I mean, Samantha is the *boss* after all, so I think she would be the most appropriate person to show me my new living quarters. Don't you? No mixed messages, or misunderstandings there."

"Fine." Geri pouts at me, and I really find this woman pathetic, and unattractive. I'm sure she gets plenty of attention with this kind of performance, but she won't be getting anything from me. She looks at her watch, and curses under her breath. "Poop, I have to go, or Sylvie will be pissed at me."

"Language please Geri." Sam warns Geri, who huffs.

"There's only us in here *Samantha* ."

"A guest could enter the foyer at any time, and if you can't remember to be professional when you're on the premises of Sandy Cove, then you'll find yourself not required to be here." I force myself to hide the smile that is trying to break free, while Geri's eyes widen in surprise.

"You heard her threaten me, right Tom?" Geri asks me, fluttering her eyes at me.

"Threaten? No, what I heard was a manager asking for respect, and professionalism while an employee is on site. I don't think that's an unreasonable request."

"I should have known you two would stick together. Management always does." Geri says rolling her eyes. "I was hoping you'd be different, but it doesn't matter how attractive you are if you're going to side with management, I'm not interested."

"I *am* management Geri." I remind her, with a shake of my head. "By the way, it's Tomas or Mr Jenson to you."

"Wh-what?"

"My name. It isn't Tom, only people who know me really well get to call me Tom, and that's not you." I hope that Sam reads between the lines, and remembers what I said to her before she booked it out of my place this morning.

"Fine!" Geri turns away from both of us, and storms out of the building, hopefully heading towards the spa, where she's supposed to be.

"Wow! She's a piece of work isn't she?" I ask, turning to around to find Sam no longer standing behind me. Damn the woman moves fast when she wants to. "Sam?" I call out, making my way into the office that I signed contracts in what seems like days ago, but was only last night. "Samantha, are you OK?" I ask, when I find her sitting behind the desk with her head in her hands.

It would seem that her transition to boss lady isn't going as smooth as I first thought.

Chapter Eleven
SAMANTHA

"Thank you." I mumble into my hands, not wanting to face him after that embarrassing display. That was mortifying on so many different levels.

"You're welcome." His voice is as sexy as I remember it, and I was hoping that in the cold light of day, that it really wouldn't be. "Can you look at me please? Sam, I don't like talking to the top of your head."

"Samantha." I say, not lifting my head.

"What?" I sigh, deeply. He's not going to let thing go, so I have no choice but to confront the situation head on. Right?

"Samantha." I say, as I drag my eyes up from the desk to meet his. "My name, it's Samantha."

A frown spreads across his handsome face. "I know what your name is, Samantha." The way he says my full name sends another fucking shudder through my body. God damn it, I'm screwed aren't I? "I just prefer calling you Sam." He pauses, before continuing with, "When we're alone."

"Damn it all to hell!" I yell, before closing my eyes, and taking another deep breath to bring myself back under control. I will not let this man, a man I've known for less than twenty four hours, screw up everything I've worked for here. "When we're here, at work, you'll call me Samantha."

"That implies that I'll see you outside of the working environment." He says, a wicked smile spreading across his lips. Lips I desperately want to kiss again, and feel all over my body. Again! "I wouldn't complain about that turn of events, sweetheart."

"It implies nothing of the sort, Mr Jenson. It means that while we are at *work* you will show me the respect I have *earned* by working my tail off, and getting Bettie to mentor me." Placing my hands on the desk, I push myself up out of my chair. "Now, as much as I've enjoyed our chat, if there's nothing else

50

you need, I need to get back to work." I look towards the open door, trying to indicate that's where he should be heading.

"I need to talk to you actually."

"Listen." I interrupt him. "I appreciate your help with Geri, but honestly, I can handle her myself in the future." I lower my voice, so that anyone passing can't hear me. "As for last night, it was exactly that, the past. You don't owe me anything, and I don't owe you anything. We were both drunk, or at least tipsy, and it happened. We're human, we were attracted to each other, and it happened."

"You're attracted to me?" His hands are in the pockets of crisp navy blue cargo pants, and he rocks on his feet, a cocky smile spread across his face.

"That's all you take away from what I just said? Seriously?" I shake my head, I don't think I will ever understand the way the male brain works. To be honest, I'm not sure I want to.

"I'm sorry that you being attracted to me means something to me." He says, shrugging his shoulders. "It means that I'm not alone in this."

"Oh you are most assuredly in this 'thing', as you call it, all on your own." I tell him in a voice that brooks no argument.

"I can *assure* you Ms Holt, I am not even close to being on my own in this thing that I call attraction, and I'll prove it." I'm nervous, and I shouldn't be.

"Don't you have some work to do, Mr Jenson?" I ask, my tone harsher than I was going for.

"I do, but first I need to ask you something."

"No." I say firmly, not waiting for whatever crazy question he's got on his mind.

"No? You didn't even let me say anything!" He says, but he doesn't sound shocked, just amused.

"Whatever it is, the answer is no. No I won't got bungee jumping, no I won't go skydiving, no I won't ride a bike around the island, no I won't go out with you. Ever." I sound like a cold hearted bitch, even to myself, but he brings out the worst in me. He also brings out the best in me, but this is definitely the worst part.

"Nice to know your boundaries, I can work with those." He nods thoughtfully like I just gave him a list of things we can't do to together, but he'll work out a list of things we *can* do together. "Nothing extreme, I got you covered Sweetpea."

I growl, actually damn growl at him! "Go get some work done, instead of harassing me."

"That is one sexy growl you've got there, but I really do need to ask you something before I jump into getting some work done."

"What is it?" I give in, because I figure this is the easiest, and fastest way of getting him out of my office so that I can get some work done.

"I'm not sure I'm liking this grumpy tone you've got going on now." He says, trying to look me up and down, but I'm sitting behind my desk. Thank god for that, because my hands are clasped so tightly together under the desk, that my knuckles are turning white.

"What. Do. You. Want. Tomas?" I ask through gritted teeth.

"Geez, you're really grumpy when you don't get enough sleep." He leans over, like he's telling me a secret, and says, "Duly noted, I'll make sure you get enough sleep next time."

"There will *be* no next time Mr Jenson. Now what is it that you wanted to ask me?" I feel like I'm about ready to explode.

"I was wondering. The bungalow." He pauses, and I swear it's purely for dramatic effect. "From last night? Is that still an option for me?"

"What do you mean?" I ask, surprised. "You want to stay there now?"

"Yeah I kind of like it. It holds some great memories for me, *and* the place I was going to stay in kind of fell through." For a second I'm pissed about his great memories line, but when he says the place that he'd already arranged fell through, I feel like a bitch.

"If you're asking if anyone else is planning on staying in there, the answer is no. We are planning on fixing up the rest of them for staff housing, because they're a little further away from the guests, giving a little more privacy, and separation for staff."

"So, I can live there like Bettie planned then?" He sounds so unsure of himself, and it's an unusual feeling, but I like it.

"I don't see why not. I'll just have to let housekeeping know that you're in there, did you want them to clean up in there for you, or do you want to do that yourself?" I pull out a notepad, and start writing notes down.

"I'd rather do it myself, if that doesn't break any rules, of course?"

"No that's perfectly fine. I like my privacy, so I keep my place clean myself." I smile at him before I can stop myself, but quickly go back to business only. "I'll let the staff know that you're in there from today. It's been empty for a few weeks, so who knows who has been sneaking in there to do what while it's been empty. By telling them, we'll hopefully be able to head those activities off at the pass." I realise what I've said a second too late.

"I think you, and I both know what happens in that bungalow by the beach, don't we Ms Holt?" He sends another god damn sexy smile in my direction, and turns towards the door. "I like that bungalow, it holds some of my favourite memories. I think I'm going to like it here." He announces, and then he's gone. I'm so dumbstruck, I can't speak.

I'm screwed. I'm so fucked if he stays here. I need find a way to get him to quit. Go running back to the mainland, and never come back!

I could encourage Geri to go after him. No, that makes my stomach churn, and my chest ache. I couldn't bear it if he decided that he wanted Geri after all.

I'm going to have to come up with another plan, or two. I don't think he's going to be very easy to get rid of, but I know when I put my mind to something, I can get it done. Even if I have to work my way from plan A, all the way through to plan Z, I *will* succeed in getting him to give up on anything else going on between the two of us.

Thank goodness we have that loose fraternisation policy, because it means he can't date Geri either. That knowledge puts a smile on my face until the end of the day. A day which was suspiciously absent of a certain Tomas Jenson after he left my office. Where the hell did he go, and what was he doing when he got there?

Leaving my office, I cross the foyer to the small room that Bettie managed to squeeze a desk, a chair, and few small pieces of furniture into, and called it the Adventure Manager's Office. What I find is, hard to describe.

Chapter Twelve
TOMAS

After sitting at my new desk all day working my way through paperwork, contracts, people of interest, and all kinds of other things that Bettie thought I might need in this venture, I'm dying to get out of here. I'm not used to being cooped up inside for this many hours of the day, and it's starting to make me feel a little crazy. I'm longing for a little sunshine on my skin, and fresh air in my lungs!

Taking a deep breath, I rub my face with hands, and let out a long, low growl.

"Is everything OK in here?" I hear her voice ask, but I leave my hands covering my face for a few more seconds, because I need to control my feelings before I look at Samantha, and give her an answer.

"Everything is just fine. Peachy keen jellybean." I tell her, moving my hands and placing them in my lap, giving her a huge reassuring grin. It may not be genuinely reassuring, but it seems to work.

"Peachy keen jellybean?" She asks, with a quirk of an eyebrow. She looks so damned adorable when she does that, but I'm never confessing that to her.

"It's a quote from an old movie that my sister used to make me watch." I tell her, waving my hand dismissively. "What can I do for you, Ms Holt?" I don't want to sound like an uptight idiot, but this is how she wants it.

"I know exactly which movie it's from *Mr Jenson,* you knowing it, and quoting it just surprised me, that's all." I can see a smile twitching her lips, trying to spread across her face, but she just won't give in. "I came to see if everything went well for you today, and to see if you needed any help. I know the paperwork that Bettie left for you might be a little overwhelming, but she's a stickler for having everything written down, just in case you hadn't noticed."

I rub my hand over my face again, letting out a quiet chuckle. "Yeah I've noticed that. I think I've used more ink, and paper today than I've used in the last five years. Didn't you tell her that it's all done online, on computers these days?"

"I tried to." She lets out a quiet laugh of her own. "But she seems to be stuck in the past. So many things I've managed to get her to change around here, but that's just not one of them. She told me I can do things my way, and she'll do them hers. When I explained that just doubled our workload, she told *me* to give up *my* new-fangled ways then."

"Right." I chuckle again, because I can imagine these two women arguing over whose way is the right way until the sun goes down, and neither one of them giving an inch. "So, now that you're in charge, can we expect to see at least a few things change around here?" I ask, hopefully, and she must see the hope in my eyes, because she laughs loudly this time.

"You know just because you looked so hopeful just now, I want to say no, I'm keeping things the way Bettie wants them, but I can't do that to you. I just can't dash the hope I can see in your eyes." She says with a shrug. "So yes, a few things will be changing and getting updates over the new few weeks, and months, but these things are going to take time."

I nod in understanding. "What are the first things you're looking at making changes to?" I ask, wondering if could help her out with any of them.

"Payroll will be the first thing I get stuck into." She answers quickly, and I know she's been thinking about making these changes for a while, just by the look of determination on her face. "Not that it would affect either of one of us, because we're on salary, but for the other staff members who are on a wage, it should make their lives a lot easier. It should also make our managers' lives easier, because they'll be able to tell who's worked, and keep hours even."

"So, you're going to online logging in, and out for shifts?" I ask, even though I think I already know the answer.

"Yes." It's a simple answer, and she really doesn't need to elaborate.

"Well, if you need any help, let me know. I helped the last couple of places that I worked get their electronic payment systems up and running." I explain, not thinking for even a second that she's going to ask me, of all people, for help.

"I might just take you up on that, Tomas." She says with a smile, and then seems to catch herself, and a serious look settles back into place. "Although, most of the work is done now." Of course it has, I knew she wouldn't want my help.

"The offer is there, if you ever need it." I say, looking back down at the papers in front of me. My brain won't concentrate on anymore paperwork, I know this, and yet I keep looking blankly at the page so that I don't have to look up into her beautiful green eyes. "Is there something else you needed Ms Holt?" I ask, my voice coming out harsher than I meant it to.

"What?" She asks, and I think she's shocked by my behaviour, I know I am, so she has every right to be. We were talking nicely, if not warmly, to each other just a second or two ago. "Oh no, I just wanted to make sure you were settling in OK, and didn't have any questions. I'll leave you to it, if you don't. Have any questions or issues that is." She turns to walk away.

"I do have one question." I say, just loud enough for her to hear. She turns to look at me, and waves a hand for me to continue. "Have dinner with me?"

"What?" She wraps her arms around her waist, and looks completely shocked that I asked.

"Have dinner with me please?" Her mouth opens, and I remember what it's like to taste those lips, and I know I want more. "Before you get ready to decline my invitation, it's purely business. I would like to get to know the restaurant, the staff, and the menu. Who better than the boss to show me all of those things?"

"So, this isn't a date?" She's cautious, and if I was her, I would be too. Is this a date? Maybe not to her, but in my mind, hell yes it is.

"Purely business." I answer, shaking my head. "No pleasure. None whatsoever, and if we start to enjoy ourselves, I promise to pull that crap back. No laughter, or fun, just a simple dinner getting to know each other. On a business level. Of course!"

"You're making me sound like I don't know how to have fun, Tomas." She frowns at me.

"I think we both know that's not true, Samantha. You are *far* from boring love bug." I grin at her.

"What's with all the different nicknames?"

"Whatever do you mean?? I ask, trying to sound innocent.

"First you called me Sweetheart, then Sweet*pea,* and just now you called me Lovebug." I watch as she crosses her arms over her chest, and lets out a very heavy, very annoyed sigh. "Tomas."

"Hmmmmmm." I can't find words, as my brain short circuits a little because her arms are under her boobs, giving them a lift, rather than on top of them, holding them down. My mouth waters at the memory of how they taste rolling around my mouth, and on my tongue. I really hope I'm not expected to stand up any time soon, because it's going to be embarrassing.

"*Tomas.* Are you OK?" The question comes out as genuine concern for my welfare, and she starts to move closer to the desk. I can't let her see the hard on I'm sporting under the desk, she'll question my professionalism.

"I'm fine. Nothing to see here. What did you ask?" I speak so fast she stops in her tracks, confusing all over her beautiful face.

"The nicknames? Why are you using them, and different ones too."

"I'm trying to work out which one suits you. Which one rolls of the tongue easier when I think of you." I answer her without thinking, and I know the minute I see her entire body stiffen that I've done the wrong thing, and I *should* have taken a minute to think about my answer. "They're all terms of endearment, and I'm just trying to find the one that fits you."

"I don't need a *term of endearment* from you or anyone else for that matter, thank you Tomas. Samantha or Ms Holt is just fine in my book." She turns to leave, and I speak once again without thinking.

"We're still on for dinner though, right?" There's so much hope, and unbridled happiness in it, I feel like an idiot, but I'm sure she can't say no to me. "Sam?" I shorten her name to ask her in a low and grumbly voice, and her body stiffens impossibly more, but she doesn't turn around to answer me.

"Of course, *Tomas.* It wouldn't be *professional* to cancel at this point." Then she's gone, and I'm letting out a breath I didn't even realise I was holding.

It's going to be tough around here if I can't get her to surrender to this attraction between us. Giving up on us isn't an option. Not for me anyway. I think I'm already half in love with the woman, so there's no way I'm giving up. I'm not going to be creepy, or stalk her or anything, but I am going to keep trying to change her mind about going on a few dates with me to see where this could go. I refuse to let a good thing pass us by, because of some perceived rules that no-one else seems to go by. I smile to myself.

I smile to myself, because I'm having dinner with Samantha Holt tonight. Just as I think that I get a message on my phone.

Unknown number: I booked us table at 6.30pm, I hope that's ok?

Me: Who is this?

Sweetness: You know exactly who it is, and I expect you at the restaurant at 6.30 tonight, otherwise I'll dine alone.

Me: How did you get my number Ms Holt?

Sweetness: Employee records.

Me: Well colour me shocked! I didn't think you'd invade my privacy like that!

Sweetness: I didn't, this is a business meeting, and therefore I didn't use the information inappropriately.

Me: I have a new nickname for you

Sweetness: No, you don't. See you at dinner.

Me: See you soon, Sweetness

Sweetness: It's Samantha or Ms Holt to you, I won't answer to Sweetness, Sweetheart, or anything else.

Me: See you at dinner Ms Holt

When I don't get message for a minute or two, I decide I'm not going to. I finish up reading the paper in front of me, clean up the small mess on my desk, and then decide I'm done for the day. Checking my watch, I realise I've got time to go back to the bungalow, and freshen up a little. I know it's not a date, but it won't kill to make a good impression, will it?

"Hey, Tomas do you have a minute?" Max says loudly behind me.

"Nope, not right now." I say over my shoulder.

"Where are you off to in such a hurry?"

"Dinner."

"You've got a date already? Geez you move fast!" He sounds surprised.

"Nope, it's business." I don't slow down as I reach the door.

"Hey Tom?" I stop and turn to look at him, because the tone in his voice seems to demand it. "Be gentle with her, OK? She's been hurt before, and if you hurt her, I'll have to kick your arse, and I don't want to do that 'cause I kind of like you."

"I'll let you kick my arse if she gets hurt, how about that?" I ask him, with my hand on the door, and he laughs.

"Sure, you'll *let* me!" His laughter cuts short, and he's deadly serious again. "I will pummel you if you hurt her."

I gulp down a swallow, and nod in acknowledgement, then I'm out in the last rays of sunshine for the day, and I already feel more energised.

Chapter Thirteen
SAMANTHA

I can't believe I agreed to this dinner. Even more, I can't believe I'm standing here staring into my wardrobe wondering what to wear! It's not like I'm going on a date, it's a business dinner.

A dinner that feels like a date that's thinly disguised as a business dinner.

"How the hell did I get talked into this one?" I ask the empty room. I know exactly how it happened. Tomas told me he wanted to ask me some questions about the resort, knowing full well I wouldn't agree to go on a date with him. He knew I wouldn't be able to resist talking about work, and he still gets to take me out for dinner.

I sigh, deciding to wear a yellow, flowy summer dress with small white flowers all over it. I pull my hair back into a loose braid, and apply some light makeup. I don't want Tomas to think that I put any extra effort into getting ready for dinner.

As I'm pulling my sandals on, there's a loud knock on my front door, making me jump a little.

"I wonder who that is." I ask out loud to the empty room, then shake my head, because if the person on the other side of the door can hear me talking, they're going to think I'm crazy.

My mouth opens to speak as I open the door, but when I see the man standing there, the words get stuck in my throat.

"I thought we could walk over together." Tomas says, with a lopsided smirk that makes a dimple appear in his cheek. How have I not noticed that before? I guess it's because I've barely known him for twenty four hours, and for at least some of those we were asleep.

"Why are you here?" He chuckles, because we both know he's already answered that question, and I want to kick myself for showing him how much he rattles me. "I mean, how did you know where to find me?" My question earns me another throaty chuckle that does things to me that I don't want to think about, because last night can't happen again.

"There aren't as many staff living on site as I thought there was. Your fine self, and Bettie made it sound like there was a thriving staff community living here, but I found out between asking you to join me for dinner, and now, that's not quite the case, is it?"

"I'm not sure what Bettie told you, but I never once said there was ... what did you call it? A thriving staff community living here at Sandy Cove? What I said was, we were planning on fixing up the bungalows in the area you're in now, to give staff somewhere to live or stay for a night or two, if they need to." I know I'm being defensive, but he's accused me of lying to him! He holds his hands up defensively, but that freaking smirk is still plastered on his face.

"I wasn't accusing you of anything Sweet Samantha ." I can't help screwing up my face in distaste over *that* nickname. "You're right, that one was horrible, I won't use it again."

"Please don't." I ask him, as he shakes his head, still laughing that low, deep laugh of his that makes me want to climb him like a tree. "That one was terrible."

"But the other ones, they were OK then?" He asks, his hands in his pockets, that dimple popping smirk on his face, and rocking on the balls of his feet.

"No." I tell him, knowing that I need to fight this attraction I have to him. I don't know what it is about *this* man, but it's like my body just gravitates towards his. It's like my body needs his to survive. "Samantha or Ms Holt is just fine." I say a little too crisply, as I reach for my handbag, and sunglasses.

"What about Sam?" He asks, stepping away from my door so that I can step out, and lock it behind me.

"No." I swear that I know without thinking about it too hard, that if I give this man an inch, he's going to take a mile, and I'll never get that back. "Samantha or Ms Holt." I tell him, and start walking towards the main building of the resort where the restaurant is housed.

"Where are you going?"

"To the restaurant." I say, without breaking my stride, or turning to look at him.

"Then you're going in the wrong direction, Snookums." I stop walking, and turn to look at him, one eyebrow raised. "You're right, that one sucks as well."

"You don't need to find me a cute pet name, or whatever you want to call it, Tomas, it won't be needed. I've told you what to call me, and I won't be answering to anything else."

"If I call you Samantha, will you actually let me take you to where I have dinner planned, or are you insisting still that you know where we're going?"

"We're not going to the restaurant here?" I ask, surprised.

"I didn't think you'd want to be seen here, with me." He admits, shoving his hands back into his pockets, and pushes his foot through the sand in front of him.

"Why wouldn't I want to be seen with you here? It's not a date Tomas, it's a business meeting." His confession that we're not eating here, and why, confuses me. "We don't owe anyone an explanation Tomas, we're allowed to have a meal together."

"I know that, but you made it sound like it would be scandalous for us to be seen together outside of office hours."

"I'm sorry you feel that way. I'm sure that there will be plenty of times that we have to work together outside of normal business hours Tomas. Tonight is about business, and I'm sure you're used to a nightlife of some description on the mainland that you won't find here. I also assume, that you haven't created a circle of friends in the last twenty four hours, and you would like some company."

"You make me sound pathetic Samantha." Before I realise it, he's closed the distance between us, and his front is almost touching mine. Suddenly, I'm finding it a little hard to breathe, and concentrate on what he's saying. "I don't just want *any* company, Sam. I want *your* company."

"Why?" My question comes out on a whisper that I'm not sure he heard.

"I don't know. I just know I want to spend time with you, and get to know you."

"It's just because I keep saying no."

"You didn't say no last night." He says so quietly that I'm not sure I heard him correctly.

"I should have."

"But you didn't."

"I was drunk."

"No, you weren't. Stop making excuses gorgeous, and admit that you feel this pull, this attraction that sizzles between us." I don't even notice his hand has moved, until I feel him tug at the braid that hangs down my back.

"Tomas." My voice is harsh, raspy whisper that I've never heard before.

"Samantha." He leans in close to me, and I think he's going to kiss me, which would be a bad thing. Right? Remind me why. Instead of kissing me, he leans in to whisper in my ear, and the hot rush of his breath on my skin makes me shiver. "Tell me you don't still want me. Tell me you don't feel this attraction, and I'll leave you alone, but I don't think you can tell me that. Not if you're being honest."

Right here, in this moment, I want to tell him yes. Yes I feel it. Yes I want him. I close my eyes, take a deep breath to agree with him, to tell him that we can skip dinner, and go back to his bungalow. Or mine, but then I hear voices in the distance, and I remember where we are. I take a large step backwards, and he drops his hands to his side.

"No."

"No?" He asks, I can see the defeat written all over his face.

"NO, I don't feel any of it. What I can give you is friendship Tomas. We have to work together, and I want to make that work, but we can't sleep together again, but we can be friends."

"Friends?"

I nod. "That's my offer, yes." I smile at him, even though I don't want to. Even though I want to admit it, with every part of my being, that he's right. I feel it too, I won't.

"OK." He nods once, and this time, I do give him a genuine smile.

"Let's go enjoy a meal together then. Did you still want to leave the resort? Did you book somewhere?" I ask, all the words melting into each other.

"No, I didn't book anywhere, because I thought you could take me to your favourite local place. Yes, we can stay here, if you're comfortable with that?"

"My favourite local place is here." I tell him, my smile getting bigger.

"Of course it is." He laughs.

"There are few small local restaurants that I love too. I'd love to show them to you one day."

"You've got a date." I frown at him, but before I can respond, he holds up one hand. "I know, it's not a *real* date."

I feel lighter, happier now that we've come to an agreement.

Chapter Fourteen
TOMAS

We get a few curious looks when we walk into the Sandy Cove restaurant, and are seated together, but no-one says a word. I think Samantha is more respected than she thinks. Either that, or they're too scared to question her, which should worry me, but it doesn't.

"What's so funny, Tomas?" Samantha asks me, and I can hear the curious amusement in her voice. She wants to know, but she doesn't like that she wants to know. She's a complicated woman this one.

"I was just wondering what kind of boss you were, that's all." I answer her honestly.

"And what was your conclusion? Or do I not want to know the answer?" I'm saved from answering her rapidly fired questions, by the waitress coming over to take our orders.

"Miss Holt, Mr Jenson, what can I get for you two this evening?"

"Good evening Sasha, how are you?" Samantha asks her with a sweet smile. There's a smile I wouldn't mind seeing directed my way every now, and then.

"I'm very good Ms Holt, thank you for asking." Sasha smiles warmly back.

"Are you sure?" Samantha inquires, a small frown on her face.

"Yes ma'am."

"What did I tell you about the ma'am and Ms Holt stuff, Sasha?"

"I remember Ms – sorry, *Samantha,* but I'm at work now, and you're not just the boss, you're also a customer. Therefore, I'll call you Ms Holt." Sasha says with a friendly smile.

"Fair enough." Samantha gives in with a quick nod. "This is Tomas Jenson, the new Adventure Specialist."

"Nice to meet you Sasha." I smile at her, and I see Samantha's smile falter out of the corner of my eye.

"Do you know what you want to order, Tomas?" She asks, her voice back to the curt tone she seems to enjoy using when it comes to me. I'd love to tell her that I have indeed decided exactly what I want, but I don't think she's ready to hear it.

"I do." I say, without looking at Sam, and talking to Sasha, I give her my order. "Your turn." I say, finally looking Samantha's way, and I can almost *see* the anger coming off her, and I struggle not to laugh.

As soon as Sasha is out of hearing distance Samantha's admonishing me. Does it make me a sick bastard that I enjoy her telling me off? It probably does, but I don't care.

"That was a bit rude don't you think?" She hisses at me.

"What was?" I bat my eyes her way, and try my best to look innocent.

"Ordering before me for one, and flirting with another woman, while sitting at a table with *me.*"

"Well, you've been pretty clear about this being a business dinner, and not a date." I say with a shrug.

"That doesn't mean you should flirt with someone else."

"I wasn't flirting with Sasha, I barely know her. I ordered my meal, Samantha, that's it. Believe me, if this was a date, I wouldn't flirt with another woman. You asked me if I knew what I wanted to order, and I took that as an invitation to do just that. Order my meal." I tell her, schooling my face, because I can feel my frustration building, and I don't want to give her another reason to write me off as a potential date. Sasha floats back our way, stalling any further conversation, to drop drinks at our table. "We didn't order any drinks."

"No, Jack sent them over." Sasha informs us, while both her and Samantha laugh.

"What's so funny?"

"Nothing really. Jack likes to think he can tell what a person wants to drink on any given day. It's become a bit of a joke among the staff, and we never order a drink any more. We only drink what Jack sends over." Samantha explains. "He probably remembered what you had last night at Bettie's party." She explains, nodding at the glass that Sasha put in front of me.

"I only had one drink last night." I say, pointedly, and I know she understands my point when I see a blush creep up her neck.

"He's got a brilliant memory for these things, and does a great job of knowing what you need to drink on any given day as well." Samantha's voice is overly bubbly, and I can tell she knows *exactly* what I mean.

"He really does have this uncanny knack of just knowing doesn't he?" Sasha says dreamily. "I'll leave you to it. If you need anything else, let me know." Then she's gone.

"I don't think you need to worry, even if I *was* flirting with Sasha, I think it would have been a wasted effort. She's got a thing for the amazing all drink knowing bartender." I say with a wink, and then I raise my glass in salute to the man in the question, who salutes back at me, before turning his attention to Sasha who is putting in another drink order.

"I doubt that would stop you from flirting." Samantha mumbles. I don't bother defending myself, I doubt it would make a difference, so I decide to change the subject to something more comfortable.

"So, why don't you tell me about Sandy Cove, and your plans for it now that you're in charge?"

"Didn't you do your research before you took Bettie up on her job offer?"

"I did, but I would like to hear about it from you, and only you can tell me the plans you have to improve the place."

"You think it needs improvements?"

"I think you can always improve, Samantha. If you don't, things become stagnant, and that's not how a successful business runs." Sasha approaches the table with our meals, and places them on the table, then disappears almost as quickly as she appeared. "So, come on, tell me all about it." I encourage her as we start to eat.

"Are you sure?" She asks after a mouthful of her dinner.

"Of course." I wave my fork in the air for her to speak, and I watch fascinated, as she starts talking about Sandy Cove, and her face lights up. She is honestly the most beautiful woman I've ever seen.

We eat dinner, have another drink, and order dessert, all while Samantha tells me all about Sandy Cove, and all the changes she wants to make. She has some amazing ideas, some of them that can be incorporated into what I'm going to do here as well.

"Ohhh geez Tomas, I've talked your ear off." She blushes as we both finish the last mouthful of our respective drinks. "You should have said something!

I'm so sorry, but once I start to talk about Sandy Cove, and all my plans, I get over excited. I know it can be overwhelming."

"Don't apologise, I love that you're so invested in the resort, and I can tell that you love it here."

"I truly do." She admits with a shy a smile. It's a new look for her, with me anyway, and I like it.

"Are you ready to go?" I ask.

"Oh, yes of course. If you're ready we can get out of here." I don't want my time with her to end, but I also know we can't sit here all night, the staff will want to go home soon, and I don't want them to feel like they can't throw the boss out so that they can go home. I know that Samantha would hate that too.

Samantha insists on splitting the bill, but she doesn't get the chance, because I just pay for the lot, and then guide her out the door with my hand on her lower back.

"You didn't have to pay." Her voice is so quiet, I can barely hear it.

"I know, but I did." I say simply, as we walk along the path to the bungalows.

"OK, well, I guess I'll see you in the morning." She says when we reach the fork in the path where her bungalow is one way, and mine is the other. "Goodnight, thank you for dinner." Obviously, she's made the decision for both of us that this is where, and how the night ends. "What are you doing?"

"Walking you home."

"Oh you don't have to do that. I've done it a million times before, and it's not even dark yet."

"I know. I also know that this definitely isn't a date Samantha, but I'm still going to walk you home. Before you argue, let me just tell you that my mother would kill me if I didn't." I raise my hands in defence. Would my mother kill me for not walking a lady home? I have no idea, but it sounds like something a mother would say. "We don't have to talk, I just want to walk you home."

She seems to have an inner dialogue with herself, and decides it's better to humour me, than argue for a change. We walk along, side by side, not talking. It doesn't mean I don't enjoy spending that quiet time with her though. When we reach her door, she looks nervous, and uncertain.

"Thank you for joining me for dinner tonight. I had a great time." I rest a hand on her upper arm, and press alight kiss to her cheek. She's stunned for a minute but then she speaks, and her voice his a husky whisper.

"Thank you for dinner. I had a good time too."

"You're welcome." I smile at her, because she looks so confused by whatever thoughts are rolling around in her head. She opens the door, and walks inside. I can see she's deciding whether or not to invite me in, but I don't want that invitation. Not yet anyway, not tonight. I want her to be sure. I want her to *know* without a doubt that this, me, us is what she wants when that invite comes.

"Goodnight Tomas." Me starting to walk away seems to help her make her decision.

"Goodnight Samantha." I turn to walk away, but after a couple of steps, I turn around to face her, continuing to walk away, only backwards. " Just so you know, I'm not giving up Sam, you can't get rid of me that easily." I send my best smile her way, before turning back around, and walking away from her, not giving her the opportunity to challenge me or tell me to give up.

One day, I will get Samantha Holt to agree to go on a date with me.

Chapter Fifteen
SAMANTHA

I'm left standing in the doorway wondering what he meant when he said that he's not giving up, and I can't get rid of him so easily.

I shake my head to get out of the trance he seems to have left me in, and close the door behind me. Pouring myself a cold drink, I can't help smiling. Despite everything in me fighting against liking Tomas Jenson, I had a good time tonight. He's smart, considerate, and seems to know what he's talking about when it comes to what he wants to do here at Sandy Cove.

Walking into my bedroom, I place my drink, and phone on the bedside table. I'm still smiling as I undress getting ready for bed. I'd rather stay up watching TV or reading a book to come down from our 'non date', but I have to be up early, and we stayed out a lot later than I expected we would.

My phone chimes with a new message, so I drop the bra I was taking off onto the floor where the rest of my discarded clothes sit, and sit down on the edge of the bed to read the message. I assume it will be Sylvie asking for details of the non-date I just went on, and I have no clue what I'm going to tell her, but I look at the screen it's not Sylvie's name on the display.

Tomas: Goodnight Sugarbear, sleep well.

Me: Sugarbear?

Tomas: Trying out a new one for size.

Me: When are you going to stop?

Tomas: When I find one you like.

Me: I like Samantha.

Tomas: I like Samantha too, very much.

Me: You know what I mean.

Tomas: I do.

Me: What do you mean, you 'like' me? You don't know me!

Tomas: Are we back at school? Do I need to send you a note in class, or get my friend to tell you that I like you? Because I have to tell you, Cuddlebear, you're not making this easy on me. You know I don't have any friends here yet.

Me: That was long for a text message.

Tomas: That's all you've got? Are you going to bed now?

Me: Yes, I was just getting changed.

I'm smiling like an idiot at my phone, and I'm glad he can't see me. Without warning, my phone starts ringing, vibrating in my hand, making me jump slightly, and squeal. It's Tomas!

"Hello."

"What do you mean, *getting changed?* Are you talking to me naked?" His voice is strained, his breathing heavy.

"No, not quite." I answer him, knowing that I shouldn't tease, I'm the one who has drawn the line in the sand so many times after all, but I can't resist.

"What does that mean, *Samantha?*" He says my name as a growl, and it's so fucking hot, I almost can't answer him.

"It means, *Tomas,* that I'm sitting on the edge of my bed in my underwear." I say in a raspy but snooty voice.

"Fuck." I hear him mutter.

"Not happening."

"You can't tell me something like that, and expect me not to want to come back to you, to make us both come, baby." His voice is quiet, husky, and full of desire. I can't tell him that that's exactly what I want him to do. Come back here, and make me come until I can't walk.

"You asked a question, and I answered it."

"So, you're willing to tell me you're sitting on the edge of your bed, in your bra and panties, but we can't have a relationship of any kid, other than professional?"

"I don't have a bra on, and never call my underwear *panties.*" I tell him.

"So – that's a no to panties then?"

"Yup"

"What do you call them then?" The curiosity, and confusion in his voice is amusing as hell.

"Underwear, or more specifically knickers." I hear his rough intake of breath, and decide it's time to end this phone call. "Goodnight Tomas."

"You're going to leave me with that image? What am I supposed to do with that Samantha?" His discomfort is crystal clear in his voice, and I can't say I'm not enjoying torturing him, even though I know I have to, because this can't go anywhere.

"You can do with that *image* whatever you choose to do with Tomas, you asked me a question, and I gave you an answer, but that doesn't mean anything's changed. Nothing can happen between us, I won't let it."

"Are you seeing someone else?" Anger mixed with pain is now in his voice.

"No Tomas, I wouldn't have slept with you last night if I was seeing someone else." I admit, my voice soft. "That doesn't change the situation though. I'm just getting to where I want to be here, I can't let anything happen between us, because I won't let anyone think I'm not taking my job seriously."

"So, it's just me, because I now work here at Sandy Cove, is that what you're saying?"

"No, it's anyone, whether they're working here or not. Goodnight Tomas." I say, and end the call.

I put the phone on vibrate, because I can't just turn it off, I'm on call around here day, and night. I notice I've got a text waiting for me, and I open it hoping like hell it isn't Tomas.

Sylvie: So??????????? How was the non-date?????? I want details woman.

Me: So many question marks!

Sylvie: Answer me then!

Me: It was nice.

Sylvie: Nice? That sounds terrible! I gave Tomas so much more credit than that! He's let me down.

Me: It was a nice time, that meant two colleagues got to know each other.

Sylvie: Well, you don't mean biblically if you're messaging me, and that's a damned shame.

Me: I already told you, and him, *that can't and won't happen.*

Sylvie: Why the hell not? You're allowed to have a life you know Samantha !

Me: You know why not, and I'm going to bed. G'night.

I put a heart emoji at the end, and then decide to hell with it, and turn the damned phone off. I don't want to deal with any more calls, or messages from anyone. If there's an emergency, or I'm needed desperately, they can come, and get me. It's one of the reasons I live on site.

I need to get some sleep, and I need to distance myself as much as I can from the activities manager before I do something stupid. Like sleep with him, again! I feel like the next few months are going to test me in ways I can't even imagine right now.

Falling asleep was easier than I thought it would be. The next few months though, were more of a challenge. They were both pure heaven, and absolute hell all wrapped up in a gorgeous, just under six feet of a man with almost black hair, and dark brown eyes, package, that I dreamt of every damned night. My dreams are so graphic, and I had such a severe case of 'blue bean', that I had to go out and buy a new vibrator because I killed the one I had. I made sure to buy a rechargeable one as well.

It's on charge every damned night!

Chapter Sixteen
TOMAS

The case of blue balls Samantha left me with that night of non-date kind of date, hasn't left me in the last six months. What did she expect me to do when she told me she was sitting in her underwear talking to me on the phone? I can tell you *exactly* what I did when she hung up on me.

I had a cold shower.

It didn't help. In fact, I had to jerk off all over my shower wall. While my hand was wrapped firmly around my cock, I remembered how her pussy felt wrapped around me instead, but the only picture in my mind was one of her sitting on the edge of her bed in just her *knickers*.

Working with her for the last six months, seeing her every damned day, smiling, and laughing with everyone who she comes into contact with has been pure hell.

Every guest got her warmest smile, and welcome to Sandy Cove. Meanwhile, every time I asked her out, she shot me down without hesitation. I was beginning to think I was fighting a losing battle, but then Sylvie knocked on my office door one day. I don't know how she knew I was there, I tried to be out every day, as far from Ms Holt as possible recently.

"Knock, knock. Are you busy?"

"Hey Sylvie, what can I do for you today?" I'd asked like it was an everyday occurrence for Samantha's best friend to swing by my office for a chat.

"I thought we might have a talk about our boss, if that's OK with you?" She'd asked, not really giving the impression that she planned on taking no for an answer as she closed the door behind her, before taking a seat opposite me.

"Take a seat Sylvie. While I appreciate you might want to talk about your boss, the fact is, I'm not into gossiping, about anyone, but especially not Ms Holt. You should know that better than anyone." I told her pointedly.

"You don't have to say a thing Tomas, I just want to say something, then I'll be on my way."

"Is she OK?" I ask, suddenly concerned for Sam. I haven't been in the office a lot lately, but I'm sure I would have heard something if she wasn't well, right? "She's not sick, or anything is she?"

"What? Oh no, no, nothing like that. " Sylvie let out a small nervous laugh, the cleared her throat. "Look, the truth is, she'd kill me if she knew I was telling you anything, and I'm probably breaking about a million different best friend codes, but I can't let her hurt anymore."

"So she *is* hurt then? Where is she?" I'm confused, but I'm getting to my feet as I speak to go find her and help any way that I can.

"What? No sit your arse down and let me explain." I sit back down heavily in my chair, confused as well. "She would kill me for telling you how she feels, that's all."

"And how is that Sylvie?" I can't help feeling that Sam's best friend is about to warn me off her, and I'm not sure how I feel about that.

"I'm not going to put words in her mouth, but I think she's fallen for you. Hard." I open my mouth to speak, but no words come out. "Look, I know you feel like everything you've done over the last few months have been for nothing, but you're wrong. I can see that you're pulling back, because you don't feel like you're getting anywhere. I'm asking you not to give up."

"Why would you do that?"

"Because she deserves to be happy, and I know she wants that too, she's just got it in her head that she needs to make a go at running this place first, and that the two things can't mix. You need to prove to her that you guys can make both personal, and working relationships work. That is if you feel about her the way I think you do. If not, then I guess this is your time to give up." I don't know what to say, and she doesn't give me the opportunity to respond, because she gets up out of the chair, and walks out of my office door.

I look where Sylvie disappeared, and see Samantha standing on the other side of the foyer, staring at the open door her best friend just walked out of. I think Sylvie actually missed seeing her there, she was so intent on getting out of here before I could respond. A look of hurt flashes across her face, but just as fast, the look I've seen most days since our night together, and our non-date night, moves over her face again.

I want to chase her down, and explain why Sylvie was in here, but what would I say to her? I'm not going to drop Sylvie in the deep end by telling Sam that she was in here betraying her. Even if she does feel like it's for her own good. I couldn't do that to either of them.

So, instead of going out there, I put my head back down to work on the paperwork I need to get done before I go out to the airport to pick up our newly-wed guests.

"What did Sylvie want?"

"Hello Samantha, how are you today?" I ask without looking up from my paperwork that I'm not doing anything to.

"Fine. Hello Tomas, I'm great thanks for asking, how are you?" Before I can answer she continues. "Now can you tell me what Sylvie was doing in here?"

"Well, that's between Sylvie, and myself unless she decides to confide in you, isn't it?" I ask, still not looking up.

"Really? You're going with client confidentiality?" Slowly I look up to meet her eyes, and for just a second I see her second guess herself.

"Just because she's a member of staff here, *and* your friend, doesn't mean I'll treat her privacy any differently to any other guest of Sandy Cove or client who books one of the adventures we offer that doesn't stay here. I would have thought you of all people would understand that."

"Please Tomas." She asks quietly.

"She wanted to talk to me about something." I offer.

'And she needed the door closed?" Oh I see now.

"So, what you're really asking me is if you can trust your best friend. If you can trust *me*." I demand.

"I didn't say that."

"You know what Samantha? You've made it perfectly clear that I'm not the guy for you, so if I want to see someone else, that's my choice." I snap, feeling completely done with all the bullshit I've fought these last few months. "But so you know, I won't tell Sylvie that you called her loyalty into question, because quite frankly, I don't want her to feel like I do right now. She wasn't here for me, not even close."

"Tomas, I'm so-." I don't let her finish, I'm not in the mood to hear another apology from her. She's always sorry that she just can't say yes.

"If that's all, I've got things to do before I go pick up Mr and Mrs Harris." I say sharply, looking back down at my desk, not seeing the paperwork in front of me.

"You're right. I'll see you when you bring the newlyweds back then." I nod my agreement, because if I speak it may be words I can't take back, and if I meet her eyes again, I might regret being short with her.

There's a limit to how far I can be pushed though, and accusing me of doing something behind her back with Sylvie, that feels like it's my last straw. I've tried so hard for months, and I feel like I'm fighting a losing battle.

All those months ago I made a promise, not just to Samantha, but to myself as well. I told her she wouldn't get rid of me so easily, that I wouldn't give up. Back then I guess I didn't know it was going to take half a year to realise that I'm beat. Back then, I believed I could wait forever for her to come around to the thought of an *us*.

Months of flirting back, and forth. It wasn't one sided, she gave as much flirt as I gave, and yet here I am, six months later, still no closer to getting her to agree to just one fucking date.

As I leave to go pick up Mr and Mrs Harris, I can't help wondering if it's time to cut my losses. I'm not leaving Sandy Cove, but I think I might have to leave the thoughts of being with Samantha Holt in the past.

I snort at the irony of going to pick up newlyweds while I break my own heart as I make the decision that Bettie's husband, Patrick was right all those months ago.

I'm not enough.

Chapter Seventeen
SAMANTHA

When Tomas brought Mr and Mrs Harris back to Sandy Cove, I checked them in myself, preferring to give a personal touch to certain guests. The moment I met Mrs Harris' eyes, Makenna, as she insisted I call her, I felt a kinship with her. At least I had until the next morning when I saw her sneaking around the foyer of our main building, where my office, the restaurant, a few other amenities, and Tomas' office was. That's where she was headed, skulking around, checking to see who was watching.

She knocked quietly on the door, and Tomas opened it, greeting her with a warm, smile. Something he hadn't gifted me with in a couple of days. Makenna lifted an finger to her lips, making Tomas laugh quietly, but he also looked around to make sure no-one had seen her, before hustling her into his office, and closing the door behind them.

Does Tomas know her? Should I speak to Mr Harris, Brady, as he asked me to call him yesterday?

Makenna and Brady look blissfully happy together, so why was she sneaking into Tomas' office? I spend the next ten minutes telling myself that I'm not actually looking at the clock, or watching, and waiting for his door to reopen. When it finally does, I look over to see Makenna leave a kiss on Tomas' cheek, and he blushes!

I couldn't resist speaking to her, as she tried to sneak out the door without anyone seeing her.

"Is everything OK Mrs Harris?" My voice harsher than I meant for it to be. The woman in question jumps a mile high, and rests her hand over her heart, which was no doubt beating furiously.

"Holy shit Samantha, you scared me!" Makenna laughs, but stopped when she noticed that I'm not laughing with her. She looked back to where she came from, and then looks back at me. "You saw me in Tomas' office then?"

"Mmm hmmm." Was all that I managed to get out. I feared that if I tried to speak, I would say something truly inappropriate to a guest. Something that I could never take back.

"I was just setting up a few surprises for Brady." She said by way of explanation, and when I raised an eyebrow at her, she gasped. "Not *that* kind of surprise." When I didn't reply, she closed her eyes, took a breath, and stood at her full height, confident once again. "Look, I know my husband OK? If he had his way, we'd never leave that gorgeous bungalow this week, and I want to experience this island. I want *us* to experience the island. We can have each other all day, every day back home, mostly, but this is a once in a lifetime opportunity for us. So, I decided to sneak in here while Brady was still sleeping to organise some activities that didn't include sex. Not that I mind, because the sex is *amazing,* but like I said, this trip isn't going to happen again for us any time soon, and I want us to enjoy it, and not just from the bungalow, or our own private beach." Makenna sighed, and I felt guilty after basically cornering the woman.

"I hope he enjoys your outdoor activities then. He's a lucky man, and you're in good hands with Tomas organising trips for you. He'll take good care of you both." I smile warmly at her, hoping that I don't look like a crazy person. "Sorry for scaring you." I apologise.

Makenna giggles. "That's OK, I guess I shouldn't been sneaking around looking like I was up to no good." She pats me on the arm. "It's OK, he didn't cheat on you honey, it's all good."

"What? No!" I splutter. "We're not together. Nope." I say, stuttering over my words.

"Oh. Are you sure? Because I've watched him watching you when he thinks no-one is watching, honey. That's not a man who doesn't know what he's missing."

"You've haven't been here for long, Mrs Harris. I was checking to make sure that a guest was safe, and that my staff weren't up to anything to tarnish the reputation of Sandy Cove. That's all." I state, my boss hat firmly back in place. No more stuttering, or spluttering out words. "You should get back to Mr Harris before he realises you were missing." I say opening the door for her.

"I guess it's my turn to apologise. I'm sorry for assuming Samantha ." I nod, not trusting myself to speak, and she gives me a sad smile, then walks out the door.

"Everything OK?" Holy shit! It's my turn to jump, and I spin around, sending Tomas a glare.

"Everything is fine, except for the fact that you're trying to give me a heart attack by sneaking up on me!" My voice is the shrillest I've ever heard it, and I hate it.

"Makenna." He says, nodding to the door she just disappeared out of. "She's a sweetheart. She asked me to set up a couple of activities for herself and Brady. She doesn't want them to stay in the bungalow the entire time they're here. I'm sure Brady wouldn't mind staying in for their entire stay." He says with a chuckle.

"They do seem happy." I say, looking out the door with a wistful feeling I've never felt before.

"You'll get your happy ever after one day too, Ms Holt." I nod, accepting that we're back to calling each other by our last names. I did this, now I have to live with it. Choices, consequences, and all that.

I don't respond to him, and I hear him quietly walk away, but I don't look to see where he's headed. Instead, I walk out the door that Makenna just did, and walk down to my favourite spot.

The same old jetty that Tomas and I met on that first night.

As I take the first few steps onto it, I realise someone has taken the time to fix the rickety old jetty. It's not perfect, it still needs some work, but someone has started the work. I make a mental note to find out who the handyman is so that I can thank them.

Sitting out here always makes me feel at peace. There's something about swinging my bare feet in the clear blue water off the end of the jetty that centres me. As I sit here today, I can't help wondering why I reacted the way I did to Makenna Harris going into Tomas' office and closing the door behind her. She had every right to be in there, and Tomas had every right to have a private conversation with a guest.

I'm not an idiot, I know the answer. I've known the answer since the minute I saw him walk into the bar on Bettie's arm. I knew the answer when Geri flirted with him, and he politely ignored her. I knew the answer all those weeks ago on this very jetty. The night I walked him to his now home in the resort, and we had sex. I knew that night. I knew the next morning. It's why I left so quickly, and told him it was a mistake.

I was scared.

I haven't been with anyone since Joey and I called off our little arrangement. I keep telling myself that it's because I'm concentrating on the job of running Sandy Cove Resort, but the truth is, I'm scared of a permanent relationship. I knew Joey and I were just having fun. So did Joey. No harm, no foul.

Then Tomas Jenson walked into my resort. The one I've worked hard to make mine, even before Bettie actually retired.

"Are you OK?" Sylvie asks as she sits down beside me taking her shoes off and moving them through the water as well.

"Sure, why do you ask?" I don't look her way, even though I can feel her gaze on the side of my head.

"Because you only come down here when you need to think about something. My guess is that something is the sexy new adrenaline junkie, activities specialist, Tomas Jenson." She bumps my shoulder with hers, and smiles. "I'm right, aren't I?"

"It's such a beautiful day out here." I say, trying to dodge her question.

"It is a beautiful day, and don't try to dodge my question. Just spill Sam, you know I'm not going to give up, and you're going to give in eventually. So, let's skip some of the steps, I've got a limited time I can be away from the spa. You really don't want me leaving Geri in charge up there for too long." She shudders at the prospect, and I can't help laughing. She's right, she won't give up, and I'll give in.

"Fine." I take a deep breath, and then spill it all out. "I saw a guest sneak into Tom's office, and close the door."

"I assume the guest was female?" Sylvie asks, looking at her feet in the water. "I also assume that you made an arse of yourself, and you *assumed* the reason behind the sneaking, and closed door?"

I nod. "She's here on her honeymoon Sylvie. She was trying to set up a few 'outdoor activities' to surprise her new husband with."

"So, *not* moving in on your man?"

"He's not my *man*, Sylvie." My head snaps up, and when my eyes meet hers, she gives me a look that tells me she knows I'm an idiot. "OK, so I guess I found myself a little jealous of a guest being in his office. Alone. With him. I'm an idiot." I sigh.

"You're not, Sam." Sylvie says quietly.

"I am you know. That night, his first night here, after we slept together?" She nods, and I keep going, because I already told her about that night, and everything since. "He wanted a relationship Sylv. That night we had dinner here? That 'business' dinner? That night he told me he wouldn't walk away, that I wouldn't get rid of him that easily, but I've really pissed him off since, and I don't think I can come back from that."

"You can Sam. I've seen the way that man looks at you. He'd forgive you just about anything honey, and I think you'd do the same for him. He might be frustrated at the moment, but if you asked him out today, tomorrow, next week, next month, he would say yes. I guarantee it."

"You can't guarantee anything Sylv." It's my turn to bump her shoulder with mine. "He's different, and that scares me, Sylvie." My voice is barely above a whisper, but I know she heard, because she wraps an arm over my shoulders.

"He is, and that's why you're scared honey."

"Is everything OK here?" Both of us startle at Tomas' voice, and I can't help wondering how much he heard. Sylvie saves me from having to look up at him by answering him.

"Everything's fine here, just two friends talking about life, and how complicated it can be, that's all Tomas."

"OK." He says, drawing the word out longer than normal. "Well, if you ladies need anything I'll just be up at my hut, sorry, bungalow." He turns to walk away, and I stumble to my feet.

"Actually, you can help me with something."

"Shoot." He says, turning back to face me, that sexy crooked smirk on his face.

"Do you know who's been fixing the jetty?" I ask, thinking that he might have seen whoever it is seeing as how his bungalow is so close.

"I do." He answers with that smirk getting more dangerous by the second, then he turns to walk home.

"Are you going to tell me?" I yell at his retreating back.

"Nope." He yells over his shoulder, and a wave of his hand.

"I just want to thank them." I yell a little louder, because he's further away.

"Still not telling you." He yells, shaking his head, and then he's gone.

"Well, fuck."

"You could always follow him, and ask him Sam." Sylvie says barely holding back her laughter.

"No way. The last time we were in that bungalow, well let's just say it was the hottest night of my life, and I live on a tropical island." Sylvie can't hold her laughter in any longer. She's laughing so hard, there are tears flowing down her cheeks. "Thanks for the support Sylv." I say, my voice full of sarcasm.

"I love you Sam, but that's just too funny." She says, wiping the tears from her eyes. "You know he did that so that you'd follow him, right?"

"Well, that backfired on him, didn't it?" I ask, as I put my sandals back on my feet, and stomp back to my office, but not before I catch a glimpse of his bungalow.

I swear I can see him standing at the window watching me, waiting to see if I'm going to go running to him to find out who's fixing my jetty. I growl in frustration, and I swear I see him laughing.

I'll find out who it is without him. That'll show him who's boss. Me! That's who! I'm still the freaking boss around here.

Chapter Eighteen
TOMAS

I should have just told her it was me, but I didn't want to. I don't know why, because I've been slowly fixing our jetty, as I've come to think of it since my first night at Sandy Cove. Maybe I'm being childish, behaving like a little boy in the playground pulling on the pigtails of the girl he likes. I don't know, but seeing her all riled up, and frustrated made *me* feel satisfied. I've been riled up with sexual tension for months now, and yanking my chain isn't helping too much. Neither are the cold fucking showers every day. I've thought about going into town to find some release, but I can't bring myself to do it.

If she's not Samantha fucking Holt, then I don't want her.

I've fought off Geri's advances, so many times I feel like it should be an Olympic sport by now.

It feels like Samantha has made avoiding me an Olympic event as well the last few months, because if avoiding me as much as possible was an event, she'd *definitely* win a gold medal. She's being polite as possible when she can't avoid me, but other people have definitely noticed. Including one Mrs Makenna Harris.

I'm thinking about how to get Geri to back off once and for all, as well as how I can change Samantha's attitude towards me, when I catch a glimpse of my favourite newlyweds at the resort. I start to smile, and make my way over to say hello, when I hear yelling, and see Makenna with tears in her eyes.

They walk towards me, hand in hand, but I know from experience that looks can be very deceiving.

"Is everything OK Makenna?" I ask, giving her husband a glare I hope that he knows that I mean to knock him out cold if Makenna says so.

"It was a simple misunderstanding." Brady answers for his wife, something that I hate.

"I wasn't asking you, *Mr Harris,* I was asking Makenna if everything was OK." He answers once again before Makenna can, and it's really starting to piss me off. All I want is for her to tell me everything is OK, then I'll leave them to it, but not until I get confirmation that she feels safe. I'm concentrating solely on Makenna, and don't notice that Samantha is standing next to me until she speaks.

"Tomas, don't." She says quietly, yet firmly, wrapping her arm around mine. Her touch instantly calms me, but I'm still watching the couple to make sure things are OK, Samantha thanks them both for being so understanding, while pulling me back towards the door that she just came out of.

"Look after her Max!" I yell over my shoulder, where Max and Lee are waiting beside the four wheel drive that they're taking them out in today.

"Oh my lord Tomas, move your butt inside, now!" Samantha hisses at me.

"I was supposed to be going on that trip today." I pout at her.

"I know, and now you can stay here, and help me." She says with a sweet smile, and I smile back at her. If the consequence of me being over protective of a guest is that I get to work with Samantha, I'm not going to complain.

Once we're inside, and she's lead me into her office, closing the door behind her, she sighs.

"You can wipe that stupid smile off your face. What the hell was that about out there? Can I trust you around our guests, or am I going to have to supervise every interaction you have with them? Because I can tell you, that's going to make my life a *lot* more difficult, and I can't see it working out well, for either of us."

"I don't like seeing guys taking advantage of women. Ever." The smile is quickly wiped off my face, because I know she wants me to explain more, and I don't want to. I know I sound like a petulant child, but it's the truth, I simply don't want to get into it.

"That's admirable, but they're our guests, and you can't go picking fights with our guests."

"I wasn't picking a fight, I was just ready to fight if he was hurting Makenna." I answer her, defending my actions.

"His wife." She sighs, and I know she doesn't get it, and I can't explain how glad I am of that. "His *new* wife. Who he's been with since they were teenagers.

Who only put off getting married because her parents were killed in a horrible car accident. You mean *that* couple?"

"Just because they're married, and been together forever doesn't mean that everything is perfect behind closed doors Samantha. Maybe he's more comfortable here, *because* her brothers and father aren't here to see it. I don't *know*, and I'd rather be cautious than have another tragedy on my conscious, OK?" I know I'm getting aggravated now, and I know she doesn't understand why, but that doesn't stop the memories from flooding into my mind.

From the edge of her desk that she was leaning on, she moves quickly, and quietly over to where I'm sitting. I close my eyes so that I don't have to look at her. So that I can't see the pity in her eyes.

"What happened Tom?" It's the first time she's used my shortened name, and it's music to my ears, I just wish she was using it while we were making love, not in false sympathy.

"What makes you think –" I don't get to finish my sentence, when she crouches down so that she can make eye contact with me.

"Don't bullshit me, Tomas. What made you so aware, and defensive of women being treated badly by men? Was it your Mum? Did your Dad abuse her? Your sister that was in that situation? A friend? Is that why you never talk about your family?" Her voice is quiet, soothing, and I *want* to tell her everything.

"You really want to know everything?" I ask, bringing my eyes up to meet hers. I need to know that she's sure she wants to hear this. "It's not an easy story to hear." I warn her.

"Then I'm sure it wasn't an easy thing to live. I want to know." There's something about her, and her voice that soothes my soul like nothing, and no-one else has before her.

"Fine, don't say I didn't warn you." I sigh. "Get yourself comfortable." I nod towards her chair behind her desk, but she sits on the floor in front of me instead.

"I'm comfortable right here." She says as she takes my hands in hers, and I immediately feel at ease. "Go ahead." Her voice is still quiet, and soothing.

"It wasn't my Mum. My stepdad is an amazing man, who taught me everything he could about channelling my energy into activities that were safe outlets for my anger, and other emotions as a teenager."

"Where's your Dad?" She asks, quietly, and encouraging.

"He died in an accident when I was a toddler. I have no memories of him at all."

"Did he?"

"No. Well, not to the best of my knowledge anyway." I take a deep breath in, trying to work out how to say what comes next, and even if I want to. "She was my friend. We'd been best friends for as long as I could remember. There was never anything romantic between us, she was more like a sister to me, but guys, and girls for that matter, couldn't understand our connection. Our friendship. They didn't like it, and didn't believe that a guy and a girl that weren't related couldn't want to fuck each other blind, but we just didn't. Anyway, we stayed really close until our early twenties, when she started dating this guy, and she put some distance between us. I was hurt, but I understood. She loved this one, and wanted to make it work. When they moved in together, I was happy for her, but we saw less and less of each other. To be fair, I'd started my career in extreme sports, and didn't have a lot of spare time to spend with her. I was rarely home. I travelled a lot." I swallow, trying to find the words to explain the rest. Her thumbs rub gently over the backs of my hands, encouraging me to keep going. "We messaged each other a lot on social media, as well as in texts, but it wasn't the same, and she never sent me pictures of herself. Not clear ones anyway, and I guess that should have been my first clue. I never even suspected a thing until her Mum called me out of the blue one day. It wasn't unheard of for her Mum to call me, but it was pretty rare. Her Mum called to tell me that my friend, Emma was in hospital. My immediate thought was that there was an accident, and I had to listen to her Mum tell me through broken sobs, that there was no accident. No, her boyfriend, who had proposed just a few months ago, had beaten the shit out of her, and she was in a coma." I close my eyes, fighting the memory, but seeing her lying lifeless in that bed still haunts me today.

"Ohhhh Tomas."

"I didn't know. I dropped everything, got the next flight back, and sat next to her bed for days, willing her to come back to us. The whole time, I listened to her Mum tell me the truth about what he was doing to her. All that time, I thought she was happy, that she was putting a distance between us because that's what adults in a relationship did. The truth was, he was controlling her. Isolating her from the people she loved so they wouldn't see what he was doing, so that they wouldn't convince her to leave. Oh he started off innocently enough. Telling her to talk to me less, because no man could be friends with a female without wanting sex, and she was an idiot if she thought I *didn't* want to get in her pants. Then he got her to pull away from her parents, her sibling, her friends, and she wouldn't listen to anyone. She only spoke to me online, because *he* could check what we were saying to one another, and I didn't even *know* he was reading every fucking message."

"Tomas, you couldn't have known. You had no way of knowing." I pull my hands out of hers. I don't want her sympathy, or her comfort. Abruptly I stand up, and start pacing the small space of the office, feeling like a caged animal.

"But that's the thing. I *should* have known. I *should* have protected her. She was my best friend. She was like a sister to me, and I let her down Sam. I let her down when she needed me the most, and I will never do that again. I will never see a man even look like they're annoyed with a woman without thinking about Emma, and wanting to protect them. I want to save them all to redeem myself for not saving her."

"What happened to her?" I can hear the hesitation in her voice. She doesn't *want* to ask, but she wants to know how it ends, and I don't blame her at all.

"She never came out of the coma." I stop pacing, and focus on the picture of the ocean that Samantha has on her wall, hoping it will calm me down. It's not until I feel her hands on my shoulders that I actually feel any sense of calm wash over me. "He got charged with manslaughter, and sentenced to ten years in jail, because the judge decided to feel sorry for him, simply because it was not his intent to kill Emma, just to beat the shit out of her. His mother cried out that she was losing her son, and I sat with Emma's mum, who had already lost a daughter, even before she died at the hands of the man who was supposed to love, and protect her." Samantha's hands drop from my shoulders, and she wraps them around my waist from behind. I feel the warmth of her body as she leans against my back, resting her chin on my shoulder.

"Do you still keep in contact with Emma's mum?"

"A couple of times a year, but it hurts to talk to each other. We're reminders of happier times, of when she was still here with us." I lay my hands on her hands that are resting on my stomach. She's the first person I've told the whole story to in years.

"He did this, not you. You can't blame yourself, Emma wouldn't want you to."

"He'll get out soon."

"Is that why you came here, to the island to work, to get away from him?"

"Yes, and no. I'm getting older, my body can't take doing the competitions, and events that it used to." I laugh, because I feel pathetic saying it out loud. "The young guys and girls coming up were starting to beat me, or come close to it anyway, and I decided it was better to quit while I was ahead rather than go down in flames as the old guy trying to keep up."

"Are you telling me, we're your retirement plan?" I turn in her arms, and when I look into her eyes, I see amusement sparkling in them.

"You could say that, yes." I smile back at her, grateful for the change in subject. "Thank you."

"For what?" She asks, her arms still wrapped around my waist.

"For listening. For not judging me." I say, rubbing my hands up, and down her arms.

"No judgement here, but you're welcome. I'm always here to lend an ear." She smiles up at me, not making to move away from me.

"Can I?" I ask, looking at her lips, so close to mine I would barely have to move to kiss her. Her mouth opens slightly, and she runs her tongue along her bottom lip, nodding. I don't need further invitation, I cup her head in my hands, and drop my lips to hers. Softly at first, until I'm sure this is what she wants.

I deepen the kiss when she gasps. "Don't. *Stop.* Tomas." Against my lips, and her hands move around to my chest, trailing up over my shoulders, and threading into my hair. I'm lost in the kiss, the sensation on her mouth on mine, and we start to take it further, but then we both her voices outside her office, and we break apart.

I shove my hands in my pockets to keep from reaching out for her again.

"As an apology I'll book a fishing charter for Brady in the morning, and a spa day for Makenna. I'll make sure both activities are complete before they have to leave for their flight home." I see the hesitation on her face. "At my expense, of course."

"That wasn't what I was concerned about." She looks at me, and I think she's considering how to ask me her next question. "Would you be going on this fishing charter with Brady?"

"I'll book it with Max and Lee." I answer her, avoiding her actual question.

"That's not what I asked." She asks, as I make my way towards the door to leave.

"Yes." I sigh. "Before you say anything, I will use it as a chance to apologise for my behaviour just now, and I promise not to throw him overboard." I laugh, but Samantha doesn't. "And as way of apology to you, you can join Makenna at the spa." I raise my hand as he begins to protest. "No, she won't want to do it alone, no woman wants that, so you can take some time to relax with her. You deserve it."

I don't give her the chance to argue, because I walk out of her office, and the building. I need some fresh air. I make the call to Max as I'm walking towards my bungalow, he agrees immediately, booking in the trip. Then I call Sylvie at the spa, and make arrangements for Samantha and Makenna in the morning as well.

Knowing that's all settled, I make arrangements for a basket of goodies to be sent to the Harris' bungalow that includes the invites to both activities.

Then I sit down on my bed, and think about kissing Samantha Holt again, and I know I'm going to need yet another cold shower before I head into the restaurant tonight to make sure that Makenna and Brady have the dinner they deserve on their last night at Sandy Cove.

Chapter Nineteen
SAMANTHA

The story Tomas told me about his friend, almost broke my heart, and I felt all the walls that I've built up to keep him out of my heart, ever since he started here, crumbling down. I couldn't *not* kiss him. I felt the pain washing off him in waves, and I had the overwhelming need to comfort him. Could I have done it in a way that didn't mean locking lips with the man I've been keeping at a safe distance? Without a doubt, but in that moment, I couldn't remember *why* I needed the distance between us, nor did I want to.

The noise of people talking outside of my office bring me back to reality with a thud. There's the reminder of why I have to keep him away, but still I wanted to kiss him, and not stop. Tomas pulls away, leaving me wanting more. If I was a suspicious woman, I might assume that it was pay back, but I'm pretty certain, he was feeling vulnerable after telling me about Emma, and needed an easy escape.

It takes me about ten minutes to collect my thoughts, and I'm sitting at my desk staring at the document in front of me, when my desk phone rings.

"Good morning you've called Sandy Cove Resort, this is Samantha Holt, how can I help you?" I say automatically. A bubbly laugh that I recognise comes through the speaker.

"Well, isn't that very formal, and polite of you Samantha?" Sylvie laughs.

"You called reception Sylvie, not *my* phone, what were you expecting?" I ask, sarcasm tripping off the words.

"Are you OK?" She asks, obviously amused. "Or does this booking I have for early tomorrow morning that a certain Adventure Specialist just made have something to do with you being a little distracted?"

"He already booked it?" I ask, surprised, earning more loud laughter from my friend.

"Yes, he just called. Your fine self, and Makenna Harris will be well looked after here in the morning. I have strict instructions from Mr Adventure Specialist to make sure you show up *and* relax." There's silence for a few seconds. To be fair, I don't know *what* to say, and Sylvie is no doubt trying to find the right words to use. "So, you knew he was going to book you into the spa with Mrs Harris?" Her voice quiet, and serious.

"Yes."

"That's all I get? Come on Sam, spill." Sylvie says, and I can hear a door closing. "I'm in my office now, no-one can overhear me. What happened?"

"We kissed. I kissed him." I whisper into the phone, because admitting it out loud makes it real.

"I thought there was an altercation?" She asks, and I can't say I'm surprised that she already knows about it. News travels fast around here.

"Why did you ask me if something happened if you already knew?" I groan, closing my eyes.

"Tomas told me why he was booking a session for you and Mrs Harris."

"What did he say?" I ask, wanting to know exactly what he told her.

"Well, he *didn't* tell me about your kiss." The disappointment in her voice is clear. "But he did tell me he had a go at Mr Harris, and how terrible he feels about it. Which is why he was booking the spa treatment, and a fishing charter with the guys."

'You know everything then." I say, trying to evade anymore talk about kissing.

"No, I don't, not even close." There's a short pause, and I'm holding my breath. "Tell me about this kiss?"

"We kissed?" Yeah, it's a question.

"Yes, you did. *You* kissed *him*, so tell me what changed? Was it as good as you remember? Are you going to do it, and more, again? Come on Sam talk to me." I sigh, because I know if I don't tell her now, over the phone, she'll just storm my office, plant herself in the chair facing my desk, and not leave until I give at least *some* details.

"He explained to me why he lost his mind when he saw the Harris' argue, and well he was so vulnerable. So sexy, but sad as well, and I just wanted to comfort him." I say the words fast, hoping that she'll catch them all, and I won't have to repeat myself.

"You couldn't have just given him a quick hug? You *had* to kiss him?" She asks, with laughter in her voice.

"You know, I could have, but I didn't, in that moment I decided to kiss him. There was no thoughts behind it. I just kissed him, because I wanted to." I defend myself. "This is why I don't tell you things. You're making a big deal out of it. We heard people talking in the foyer, and he left here like his pants were on fire. Then he was right on the phone to you, so I don't think he was thinking about kissing me."

"I doubt that very much Samantha Holt. I know that night together months ago set a fire in him that's seen him consistently trying to get you to go out with him. I think you're guaranteed that he's thinking about that kiss. Especially because of the fact that *you* initiated it. Maybe after all this time, he just doesn't know what to do about it?"

"Really? He needs to think now?" I whine, knowing I sound like a child, and Sylvie laughs at me some more.

"Yes, he does. You've given him a complete cease and desist vibe, and now you've kissed him. I think the man deserves some time to consider his next move. Don't you?"

"Arghhh." I grumble into the phone. "Fine! I need to get back to work, I'll talk to you later." We say our goodbyes, and then I bury myself in the paperwork that's been sitting on my desk waiting for me.

The rest of the day goes by quickly and without incident. I only see Tomas for a short time when the Harris' get back from their trip, while we both catch up with Max, and Lee to make sure everything went well. I can't get him alone, so I don't get to talk to him about *the* kiss. Then he leaves with the guys to talk about a couple of bookings without looking my way. Which leaves me to apologise to the Harris' about earlier, on my own.

I'm exceptionally surprised when Brady easily accepts my apology on behalf of Tomas, and myself.

When Brady said, "I'm sure he has his reasons, and a guy being protective of a woman he barely knows is a pretty redeeming quality, honestly." I see the pride on Makenna's face, and he makes me rethink Tomas' behaviour. Especially since he explained his reasoning behind his outburst to me this morning.

"He does have his reasons, they aren't mine to share, but I can say that your assessment of the man is spot on. Thank you for being so understanding." There are hugs all round, and assurance that there are no hard feelings at all from our guests.

I hustle them out the door, towards their bungalow so that they can get ready for their last dinner at the resort. Tomas and I have organised a special evening for them, and we watch their enjoyment from the hostess stand.

"They look like they're enjoying their last night." Tomas says, and I swear I can hear some longing in his voice.

"We're heading out now, thank you for everything." Brady says, when they reach the hostess stand on their way out.

There's a little bit of small talk, and I can honestly say, I consider them friends after getting to know them this week.

"In an attempt to make up for my rather unprofessional behaviour I've left a couple of surprises in your room." Tomas promises them, and when they start to protest, he holds up his hand to stop them. "I swear it's not offensive, you'll both love it, and I *did* have to Makenna, Brady. It's my treat, and it would be rude if you didn't accept my generous offer."

There is a small amount of grumbling, but the Harris' end up graciously saying a polite thank you, and head back to the bungalow. I know what Tomas has in store for them, so I'm not sure why he felt the need to reassure me that it wouldn't offend them.

"What else did you organise Tomas Jenson?"

"You have a serious lack of faith in me, Samantha Holt! You should be ashamed of yourself." His voice sounds like he's offended, but there's a smile on his face that can only be described as cheeky.

"Tomas!" I growl, and I watch as his eyes darken with lust. Well fuck me if that isn't sexy as hell.

"If you must know." He says, stepping into my personal space, but still not actually touching me. "I set them up with a large bowl of chocolate covered strawberries, and a bottle of champagne. The invitations to both the spa treatments, and the fishing charter are on the room service tray as well."

"That was very nice of you." I say, swallowing nervously, because he's just so damned close to me. "Very romantic. I didn't know you had it in you." Honestly? I have no clue what the man has in him, I mean we had one night together, and I've stopped every effort he's tried since, to get me to give him more. I know

I'm not going to be able to resist him for much longer though, I can feel myself weakening more, and more every day.

"I know how to woo a woman, Samantha. You'd know that, if you just let me in." Then he turns, and leaves me standing there. Alone. I let out the breath I didn't even know I was holding.

"Please tell me you're going to give in to the chemistry between you two soon?" Sylvie's voice says, startling me. "Because I don't think the rest of us can survive it much longer."

Turning to look at my friend, I admit something I never thought I would. "I am." It's that's simple.

"Thank fuck for that!" She draws me into a tight hug, and bounces both of us around for a few seconds. "I'm so happy for you! Let's face it, that just now, was so damned hot, that I thought I'd get third degree burns just standing here."

"What about what people will think though?" I ask quietly in her ear, because she hasn't let me go just yet.

"What?" She pulls away from me, holding me at arm's length with her hands on my shoulders. "Do you mean what will *Geri* and *Joey* think?"

I nod my head. "And Bettie."

"Let's get one thing straight, Miss Bettie Bryant just wants you to be happy, and if that's with Tomas Jenson, then she'll be happy for you. Do you hear me? As for the other two, they don't matter when it comes to this Samantha. I mean, why does their opinion matter to you? Is it because you had a 'thing' with Joey, what, over a year ago now? Is it because Geri is a loudmouth, who thinks she's irresistible to every man on Earth?" I don't get to answer any of her questions, because she barely takes a breath before continuing. "Because let me tell you something, Joey wasn't in it for a deeper relationship with you. He's not ready to settle down, and I doubt he ever will be. You *both* filled a need for each other at the time. Was he upset when you guys broke up?"

"No, but I wouldn't describe what we had as a relationship." I say as she takes a breath.

"Exactly! He knew the score, and so did you. As for Geri, did you know she's been trying to get Tomas to go out on a date with her. Anywhere he wants to go, she's up for it. I've heard her tell him as much." I feel my body stiffen, because I've seen Geri in action when she's got her eyes on a man. "Do you want to know what happened, or would you rather assume you know?" She's got a glint in her eyes that I just know means mischief.

The restaurant manager chooses that moment to come over, a smile spread across his face. "Good evening ladies, why don't you two get out of here? It's quiet now, so you should head out Samantha." Sylvie speaks before I can get a word out, and loops her arm through mine, already leading us out the door.

"Thanks Andy, you're perfect, don't let that wife of yours tell you otherwise." A loud laugh sounds behind us.

"Thanks, I'll let her know you said so Sylvie." He calls out, as the door closes behind us, and Sylvie reaches her hand above her head, and waves.

"Sylvie!" I scold her, as she drags me out of the building. "I *was* going to send Andy home early to that gorgeous wife of his, until you stopped me."

"Well, now you're not." She answers simply, power walking us both towards my bungalow. I pull on her arms trying to stop our progress, because I realise she's taking us to my place. "By the way, Tomas always politely told Geri no."

"Sylvie, I have more work I could be doing in my office." I whine. Not wanting to think about Geri and Tomas.

"I'm sure you do hun, but you're not doing it. You're allowed to have time out Samantha. You remember having fun, right? And relaxing, you remember how to do that too, right?" She asks with a smile, and a raise of her eyebrows.

"You *know* I'm relaxing tomorrow morning." I say opening my door, and walking inside, and not looking to see if she's following me. "In order to do *that*, I need to get some work done. This is why it's not a good idea to date someone you work with. They distract you from your work."

"He could do that without working here Samantha, and you know it!" Sylvie admonishes me as she closes the door behind, and gets comfortable on my couch, making it clear she's staying. "What he's set up for you and Makenna tomorrow is very sweet, and thoughtful."

"Yes, it is." I can't argue with her, she's right. "Don't you have a husband to get home to?" I ask, only half joking.

"Nah, he's away for a week with work." She says, taking off her shoes, and curling her feet under her, getting comfy. "Why don't we have a girl's night, and watch a movie?"

"Sounds good. You choose the movie, I'll get snacks and drinks." I tell her, walking into the kitchen and organising everything.

"Sounds good." I settle back onto the couch, handing her a drink, and some popcorn. The smile on her face is a little bit of a worry, but she's right, I could do with a girls night in.

The RomCom she chose starts up, and half an hour into it, I understand why she was smirking at me. It's a 'co-workers get together' storyline, and it's pretty much a movie about my life!

The credits roll, and I look over to tell her she's very clever, that's when I realise she's asleep! I'm embarrassed to admit, I have no clue when she actually fell asleep either, I was completely invested in how their story would end, even though I knew that a happily ever after was pretty much guaranteed.

I clean up our munchie mess, and throw a blanket over Sylvie. Turning off the lights, I put myself to bed, leaving my phone on the bedside table. It vibrates, letting me know I've got a message.

Tomas: Goodnight Samantha. Sleep well

Me: are you stalking me?

Tomas: no

Tomas: Is everything OK. Is someone outside your house? I'll be right there.

Me: NO! Do not come here! There's no one here.

Me: Sylvie is here but that's it!

Me: I asked because I just got into bed

Tomas: Are you sure you're OK?

Me: Yes, I'm fine.

Tomas: so, you're in bed huh? Whatcha wearing?

Me: really?

Tomas: ahhh yes really!

Me: Nothing!

Tomas: I'll be right over ....

Me: No! I mean I have pyjamas on, and you can't come over. Sylvie is here

Tomas: so if Sylvie wasn't there you'd let me come over?

Me: maybe ......

Tomas: I'll take it, that's progress. Good night princess

Me: goodnight

I keep my phone in my hand for a few more minutes, not convinced that he'll give up that easily, but it seems that he did.

I fall asleep with a smile on my face, and when I wake up to the smell of coffee in the morning, I have an even bigger smile on my face.

"Good morning sleepy head." Sylvie chimes from my kitchen.

"I didn't know you were a morning person." I grumble.

"I'm not normally, but there's just something about today that's making me happy."

"Awesome. Lucky me!"

Thankfully, she leaves me alone in the kitchen to finish my coffee, while she has a quick shower, and then I have one myself.

We leave my place together, and start off in the same direction until Sylvie splits off to go to the spa, and I head towards Makenna, and Brady's bungalow.

After a small conversation, in which I embarrass myself, Makenna agrees to me joining her at the spa. I wish I'd known that Tomas hadn't even mentioned to her that I was joining her.

Sylvie greets us at the spa, and leads us to the change room. Before she leaves, she gives me a look that tells me she's apologising for something that hasn't happened yet. Then I hear Geri's voice, and realise that Sylvie had to place her as our therapist. Awesome! So much for relaxing.

Geri sets us up in the first room, and I enjoy the silence, that is until Makenna starts questioning me about Tomas, and my feelings for him. After admitting to her that we like each other, and more questions after that about the why's and why nots, I'm exhausted.

Geri comes in before we can go to the massage, and hands me a note.

"I'm sorry Makenna, I'm going to have to leave you here. Something came up at the main office. You'll enjoy your massage though, Joey is the best."

After promising to think about everything we talked about, she gathers me into a warm embrace. "He's a good guy." She whispers in my ear so that only I can hear her, then she follows Geri out of the room, and into the massage room where Joey waits for her.

I make my way back to the change room, and quickly put on my clothes, then I make my way over to the main office building where I run right into Tomas.

"I thought you were out on the boat, fishing?" I ask, not expecting to see him back yet, and the smile he sends me makes my heart beat faster.

"Did you miss me princess?"

"I just wasn't expecting you guys back so early. Is everything OK?"

"Everything is perfect." He smiles stepping into my space.

"Oh you smell." My face screws up in disgust, and he laughs.

"You're right, I'm going to go have a shower." He leans in close to ear, and whispers. "Wanna join me?"

"I can't, there's an emergency." I squeak out.

"Yeah, it's me. I'm the emergency. We're cooking lunch for Makenna, and Brady." He announces, and then he's gone, leaving me standing there in shock on so many different levels.

This man might just kill me!

Chapter Twenty
TOMAS

I love leaving Samantha standing in place, shocked. It's become one of my favourite things to do.

The fact that I smell like raw fish, and sweat is the only reason I'm leaving her today. There's a little bit extra bounce in my step though, because I realise that she missed me while I was out on the boat, but she only just now realised it. She would have made my day if she'd agreed to joining me in the shower though.

In my bathroom, I strip out of my clothes, and just as I'm about to step under the water, there's a knock on my door. I turn off the water, and wrap a towel around my waist.

With a wide grin on my face, I open the door. "You couldn't resist my invitation, could you."

"Ewwwww I would definitely resist any kind of invitation from you that meant I got to see you naked man." Max says, as he pushes by me into the bungalow, Lee following hot on his heels wearing a shit eating grin on his face, and bouncing his eyebrows up and down in appreciation as he looks me up and down. Because that doesn't make me queasy, and nervous at all. "Do we need to ask who you were hoping to see on the other side of the door when you opened it in just a towel?"

"What are you doing here?" I ask, ignoring his question, and his raised eyebrow.

"Didn't want to head home only to turn around, and come right back for lunch, so we figured we'd come to yours, maybe have a shower ourselves to freshen up." He says, dumping a duffle bag at his feet. "We smell like fish guts, you know?"

"So I've been told." I mutter.

"Ahhh now we know why you're having a shower, *and* hoping for company!" Max laughs, and Lee chuckles quietly beside him.

"Whatever." I growl out. "I'm going to finish what I was about to start, you two jokers can wait." I walk back towards my bathroom, not feeling quite as chipper as I was the first time. I stop at the door, and turn back towards the guys. "So, do you two shower together as well?" I quickly close the door, and lock it, because knowing those two, I'm not safe in here even before I joked about them showering together. I jump when I hear a quiet thump against the door as I step under the water, but I know they can't get in here unless they bust down the door, which they won't do because Samantha will kill them.

The vision of Samantha standing there looking gorgeously shocked earlier enters my mind as I wash the shampoo out of my hair, making me smile. As I start soaping up the rest of my body, I concentrate on my very hard cock that stood to attention just thinking about the object of our affection.

"Hurry up Tom! We want to smell nice too, *and* we can't leave the beautiful Sam to organise everything for lunch." I groan, and not in satisfaction either, complete frustration washes over me. "Stop playing with your dick, and hurry up!" I drop my head to my chest, I guess that's what I get for giving them grief about their showering habits.

"I'm coming." I yell out, realising my mistake a second too late.

"Too much information dude!" Lee yells back, and the fact that it's him gives me enough cause to finish up, and get the hell out of there.

Wrapping the towel back around my waist, I open the bathroom door, and head towards my bedroom without looking at the guys.

"You better move if you want to help Samantha with lunch." I say disappearing behind my bedroom door.

I hear the two of them argue, with a bit of pushing, shoving, and then Max calls out a warning to Lee as I hear the shower turn on again. "You'll keep! You better make it quick, and leave me some hot water, you fucking bastard."

I laugh at their antics, but I take my time drying myself off properly, and getting dressed. I'm not in too much of a hurry to go out into my living room when Max is the other one in the room.

"Stop putting off the inevitable, and get your arse out here, Jenson." Max calls out, and I know my time is up. Sighing, I rub my hands over my face, and I know it's time to face the music. "It's about time you came out of hiding." He says as I enter the living room at the same time as Lee emerges from my bathroom.

"What is it you need to say Max? Get it out now, and be done with it *buddy*." I say sitting in the seat opposite the couch he's sitting on, Lee joins him on the couch. The two of them together, Max the one talking for the both of them, and Lee quietly scowling, feels like the fucking firing squad.

"I'm only going to say this once Jenson, you understand us?" I nod. "You look after our girl, or you'll have us to answer to. Do we understand each other?"

"Absolutely." I nod. They both stare at me for a half a minute, and the smile is back on Max's face, and he announces he's off to have a quick shower. That leaves me sitting in my home, with Lee staring me down. "I won't hurt her Lee. Not on purpose anyway, I promise."

'OK." He says with a sharp nod, packing all his old clothes into a second duffle that I didn't see earlier. A short couple of minutes later, Max returns to the living room, packing the rest of his stuff into the duffle, both of them then toss their bags at my front door.

"Do you mind if we leave our stuff here?" Max asks, with the expectation that I won't argue.

"Sure." I shrug my shoulders. "Let's get out of here before Samantha wants to string us all up for giving her extra work to do." I brush by them to walk out the door, they're close behind me. "Lock the door would ya?" I say over my shoulder, and I hear Lee flip the lock.

When we get over to the staff barbeque area, I see that Samantha has been busy. She's already got a couple of tables set up with food, plates, and cutlery.

"What do you need us to do Sam?" Max asks, before I can, and Samantha, starts issuing orders like a professional, and that's exactly what she is. When everyone else is busy, and we've all been working on our own jobs for a while, I walk up beside her.

"Thank you for doing all of this." She stops what she's doing, hands mid movement, to look at me, her eyes darting between mine to check my sincerity. "I didn't mean for you to make this much fuss, but I do appreciate it. The boys, and I will clean everything up afterwards, you won't have to lift a finger. I promise." I smile at her, hoping that my charm can work on her.

"You're damned right you guys will clean up afterwards. I had to get this organised so quickly, that the session at the spa this morning is almost null and void."

"I'm sorry." I hadn't even thought about that.

"Just know that I'm relaxing once the Harris' get here, and you guys will be cleaning up afterwards. You won't be getting any help from me, or any of the other staff either."

Any response I could give her gets caught on my tongue as the guests of honour arrived, and I can't help smiling broadly at Brady when he catches my eye, and winks. I saw him and his wife getting a little hot, and heavy against the wall of the spa not a few minutes ago. The blush that creeps over Makenna's face tells me she knows exactly what I'm thinking about, and I laugh.

Makenna walks over to Samantha to speak to her, while I lead Brady over to where Max, and Lee are now standing. When we start chatting about the fishing trip I can't help laughing when Brady says he swore he saw his life ending the moment I approached him, and informed him I was joining them.

"The look on your face when I met up with you on the way to the jetty just about made my day, maybe even my month to be fair." I laugh loudly. "I can honestly say, I had no intention of throwing you overboard, but I do want to apologise once more for my behaviour yesterday Brady." I say seriously. "I had a friend who was the victim of an abusive boyfriend, she didn't make it out alive, and I might get a little irrational when it comes to seeing a guy get physical with a woman. Wife or not." I explain without going into details. He accepts my apology with a solemn nod.

Without another word, we've got the barbeque fired up, and we're cooking the fish that we caught this morning. When I catch Brady making googly eyes at his wife, I can't help ribbing him.

"Hey dude, are you cooking lunch or making gooey eyes at your wife?" I ask, jabbing him in the ribs.

"Cooking *dude*, but can you blame me? My wife's gorgeous and I like looking at her. Your damned lunch, is almost done so I hope you've got everything else ready to go?" Tomas smiles widely at Brady, and nods.

"Of course I've got everything else sorted and ready to go." I tell him

"You mean I got everything else sorted, and it's now all ready to go, because you did nothing, as per usual." Samantha says, making me jump slightly, because even though her voice doesn't seem to be carrying any anger, her face sure does, but I just smile widely at her.

"You like feeding me, don't you sweetness?" I ask, after leaning in close to her, and say it just loud enough that she can hear me. A shiver runs through her body, but then I'm distracted by Brady greeting someone else to lunch.

After greeting both Makenna, and Brady, Joey the masseuse turns to Samantha, who blushes furiously.

"Samantha. How are you?" He asks, with a knowing smirk. I'm trying to work out exactly what it is that he thinks he *knows*.

"Good. Thanks." Samantha stutters, when the man comes over ignoring my presence to talk to her.

Brady grabs my attention to ask a question about the fish cooking, but I'm not listening to him, because behind me I overhear Joey ask Samantha if she cooked all the food. When he casually mentions their close relationship, and how intimately he knows her cooking, I see red, but I refuse to ruin the Harris' last meal with us.

"And how the hell do you know how well *Samantha* cooks?" I ask, needing to hear the answer, but not really wanting to hear it.

"I know because she's cooked a meal or two for me, Tomas." Joey says, with an easy smile.

"You two dated?" I ask, through gritted teeth.

"No!" Samantha says, her head coming up to look at me so fast, I swear it almost flew off her shoulders. "No, we didn't date."

"No, we had more of a *friends with benefits* arrangement, didn't we Samantha?" Joey chuckles, like he's remembering all the good times they shared.

I'm left sitting at the table fuming. I have no idea what I'm supposed to do now, but I guess I've got answer to why she doesn't want to date me. She already tried that out with Joey.

Lunch is finished in awkward silence, then we all take turns saying goodbye to Makenna, and Brady. As soon as the newlyweds are out of sight, Samantha starts to clean up, but when Max tells her we'll do it, she bolts towards her office without another word.

"Go on, go talk to her Tomas." Max says. "We'll clean up out here, won't we Lee?" Lee grunts his answer, which could mean yes, fuck you, or OK. I don't give them the chance to back out from the offer, and follow closely behind Samantha.

I'm going to get some answers one way or another today.

Chapter Twenty-One
SAMANTHA

"He's the reason you don't want a relationship with someone you work with, isn't he? He's the reason you keep refusing to go out with me?" Tomas' voice demands from behind me as he slams my office door shut. The one I thought I'd damned well locked so that I'd be left alone for a few minutes to think.

"No!" I yell at him, spinning around to look at him.

"Are you really comparing *me* to that meat head? Seriously, Samantha!"

"Don't call him that!" I yell again, because if nothing else, Joey is my employee, but he's also still a friend, and a nice guy to boot, despite what he just did out there.

"Now you're defending him? Great! That's just fucking brilliant" Tomas asks, as he paces the small open space in my office.

"Get out" I say, quietly.

"No." He stops pacing for a few seconds to send a dirty look my way. "We're talking about this. Now."

"It's none of your goddamned business Tomas!" I ground out between gritted teeth.

"I'm making it my business, *Samantha!*"

"Well, you have no god damned right, so shut the hell up, and get out of my office. We've got guests to say goodbye to, and you've got a golf cart to drive."

"Fine, but we'll finish this conversation when I get back."

"No Tomas, we won't, because there is nothing to discuss. This is my life, my private life, and it has nothing to do with you. You have no say in anything that I do away from the resort, ever."

"This isn't over."

"Yes, it is. Let's go."

Tomas flings my office door open, and storms straight towards the bar, and I'm worried for a few seconds that he's going to down a shot, before getting behind the wheel of our golf cart. I know it sounds ridiculous, but it's still a vehicle.

I feel guilty when I see him snatch a set of keys out of the bartender's hands, and comes over to where Makenna, and Brady have joined me.

"Are you guys ready to go? You're our only guests that are leaving today." He says to the couple, with a smile so forced he almost looks like he's in severe physical pain.

"Just give me a second, please?" Makenna asks him and he only nods his answer. She walks to where I'm standing behind the reception desk, and engulfs me in a hug. She's soon followed by her husband, who whispers an apology that I accept without hesitation, because he didn't do anything wrong. Then we're joined by Max, and Lee as well, who I didn't even realise were in the building.

"You take care of yourself lady." Makenna smiles, her eyes a little watery.

"Let's go guys, otherwise you're going to miss your flight out of here." Tomas says softly, while reaching out for their bags, but only managing to pick up Makenna's, before Brady picks up his own, and then, they're gone.

"Are you OK Samantha?" Lee asks, Max right behind him, who is very quiet for a change.

"Yeah, I'm fine Lee, thank you. You guys should get back to whatever it is you do when you're not here." I force out a laugh that sounds fake, even to me, but they don't argue. They give me another hug each, and then they're gone.

I work out why about ten seconds after they turn away.

"Are you OK Sam?" I turn to look at Sylvie, and shake my head, afraid that if I speak, the tears will fall.

"Come on, let's go into your office." I shake my head no. "I'll get someone to cover reception. You go into your office, then I'm taking you home." I do as I'm told, because I don't have any fight left in me. I hear noises outside of my office, people talking, papers shuffling around, and then Sylvie comes into my office. I don't even know how long I've been sitting here, just staring at the wall. "Let's get you home." I let her pull me up to stand, and guide me out of the office, out of the building, and towards my house.

Sylvie lets us inside, where I sit down on my couch, and that's when the tears start.

"Oh my god Sylvie I'm so mortified!" I whine.

"Joey shouldn't have spoken about you like that. He was wrong, and I've already spoken to him about it Sam. I put him on notice, if he does anything else, he won't be working here anymore."

"What? No!" Sylvie looks at me surprised. "I mean, sure what Joey did was mortifying, but Tomas' behaviour was so much worse. How dare he speak to me like that! He has no right to be angry with me. He knew, I told him that I'd already had a workplace romance, and that I didn't want another. Especially now that I'm the boss. He has no claim on me, and even if we *were* dating, behaving like a caveman, and banging his chest like that, was completely unnecessary."

"But, Sam, honey, did he *know* that the previous relationship was with Joey?" Sylvie asks, quietly.

"Does it matter?" I scream. "It's none of his fucking business, Sylvie. I didn't ask *him* for a list of his ex's, or of people he's slept with." I throw my hands up in frustration.

"To be fair though, Tomas doesn't still work with the girls that he's had a relationship or had sex with, does he?" She asks, one eyebrow raised in question. "From what I understand of what you *have* told Tomas, you've given him the impression that the last guy is the reason that you don't want a relationship with *him,* and now he finds out, that guy is Joey. Someone you have the potential to see every day."

"But I don't see him every day. He doesn't even *work* every day." I whine even more, and I hate the sound. This earns me both of her eyebrows raised, almost into her hairline. "What?"

"You *know* what! Seriously Sam, think about this from Tomas' point of view. Imagine how *you* would feel if the situation was reversed." She holds her hand up to stop me from speaking. "I'm not saying you don't have the right to be mad him, at both of them if I'm being honest. I also think that you need to stop, and think about what just happened, and how you would feel if the situation was reversed."

"I'm not really that mad at Joey, he did the wrong thing for sure, but he didn't do it to be an arsehole."

"Are you sure about that?" Sylvie asks. "Because I've seen Joey with Geri a lot lately, and they've always got their heads together whispering, and laughing, stopping when I walk in the room. Quite frankly, I've been thinking of hiring some new staff, and slowly easing them out. I can't straight out fire them until they actually do something wrong." She takes a breath, sighing, before asking me a couple of questions that really make me think. "Are you *sure* you're defending the right guy?"

"I'm wondering if I am now." I close my eyes.

"And have you really thought about *why* you're so angry with Tomas, but so blasé about Joey's behaviour?" She pauses for a second or two. "Perhaps what Tomas thinks matters to you. Joey not so much?" She's right. She is one hundred percent right!

"Why didn't you tell me that you were having trouble with them?" I ask, ignoring her question, which earns me an eyeroll. I guess she knows exactly what I'm doing.

"Because they're mine to deal with, you've got enough on your plate." She waves me off.

"We're doing this together Sylvie, I know you're the manager of the spa, and they're your staff, but I'm the resort boss, therefore it *is* my job to back you up."

"Well, now you know." Dismissing me with another wave of her hand. "I think you've got more important things to deal with right now, don't you?" Before I can respond there's a knock on the door, Sylvie moves towards the door to answer it. When the person on the other side speaks, his voice sends shivers down my spine.

"Samantha, open the door." There's a pause. "Please?" Sylvie looks at me, questioning me without saying the words, and I give her slight nod in answer, so she opens the door.

"Samantha." Tomas starts. "Oh, hi Sylvie, how are you? Is Samantha here?" He's asking her, but the tone of his voice says that while he might have been caught off guard to see Sylvie on the other side of the door, he knows that I'm home.

"She is."

"Can I come in, and speak to her. Please?" He's not begging, simply asking. Sylvie looks back at me, and I nod. She steps away from the door, and waves her hand for him to enter. "Thank you." He says as he walks by her, and the second I see him, I realise that Sylvie was right, I defended the wrong man.

"You're welcome."

"Samantha." His voice is so quiet, I almost don't hear him.

"Do you need me to stay, Sam?" Sylvie asks at the still open door.

"No, I'm OK. Thank you Sylvie. For *everything*." I give her a smile that I hope reassures her that I'll be OK.

"Be nice to each other." The sound of the door closing quietly tells us that she's gone.

"I'm sorry." We both speak at the same time, breaking through the silence.

"You don't have to apologise Samantha." Tomas says intensely, while shaking his head.

"Yes, I do." Knowing that I owe him an explanation. "You were right, I should have never defended Joey. I should have taken the time to explain what he was talking about to you instead of launching in to defending *him*."

"It's OK. You don't owe me an explanation, Samantha." He takes a step closer to me, and I find myself stepping closer to him as well. "I had some time to think on the way back from the airport, and your past is exactly that. You've never asked me about mine, and I should have never reacted the way I did."

"No, Joey shouldn't have said anything, and I should have told him so at the time. I guess I was just so mortified by what was coming out of his mouth. No-one here, except for Sylvie knew anything about our 'relationship'. At least I didn't think so, but from what Sylvie just told me, I suspect Geri was behind Joey's outburst to a degree."

"What the hell does Geri have against you?" Tomas asks, confused.

"I think she has a couple of issues with me, least of all the fact that Joey, and I had an arrangement. I get the feeling that she'd tried before, and after that, I insisted on exclusivity while we were involved." I tell him with a shrug of my shoulder. "Other than that, she has a real problem with women having any kind of authority over her, perceived or real."

"So, basically, she's just a bitch who can't stand women who are in higher positions than her, because she thinks she deserves them?" He asks, disgust in his voice. "Can I ask you something? You don't have to answer, you can tell me to fuck off if that's what you want."

"Sure. Ask me anything. No more secrets, even by omission." Somehow, we've moved so close that our chests are almost touching.

"Were you *both* exclusive?" His eyes are darting between mine, looking for the truth.

"Yes. Obviously, I can never be one hundred percent sure of Joey exactly, but he says he was, and I believe him." He nods once. "And we always used protection. Always."

"OK."

"OK? That's it?" I'm shocked. This man never ceases to amaze me. He has shown me in so many different ways since he started here coming up to a year ago, patience, understanding, and compassion. He's been passionate about his job, and helping any, and all staff when he could. He's had my back when it came to guests, and staff. He's pursued me without being forceful, or creepy, by giving me the space to say no, while hoping for a yes, and I've knocked him back at every opportunity.

"Yes. That's it." He smiles at me. "I was being an idiot, and I won't do it again. Can I kiss you now?"

"Yes." I whisper, the anticipation of his lips touching mine again, is killing me. He moves so slowly, I almost grab his hands myself, but I stay still, looking into his eyes to see if he changes his mind. When his hands finally gently cradle my face, I nuzzle into them, my eyes closed. My desire for this man is so intense, physical, and emotional. I've fought my attraction to him for so long, that I can't hold back any longer. "Kiss me Tomas." My demand is a hoarse whisper.

Tomas hesitates for one more second, his lips almost touching mine. I can feel his breath on my lips, and his lips are on mine, gently at first, then taking control of the kiss, and demanding entry. I give in to him, and let my hands wander over his upper body. I run my hands down his sides, hooking my fingers in the waist of his jeans, and pulling his body tight against mine. My fingers skim under his shirt, and I can't resist exploring under the rest of his shirt, making him groan into my mouth.

"Fuck me, Samantha. Your touch sets my blood on fire." I smile against his lips, then pull away from him just enough so that I can pull his shirt up, and he does the rest of the work, yanking it up over his head and throwing it to the floor. He rests his hands on my hips, but doesn't pull me any closer. "Are you sure?" He asks, making me feel guilty, because I can hear and *see* the hesitation he's feeling. I created that.

"Yes." I run my hands up his chest, resting them on his pecs. "I want this, and I want *you,* Tomas Jenson." He studies my face, obviously looking for any hesitation on my part, so I smile at him, then I lean down, and kiss a nipple, while running my hands all over him. His chest, back, arms, and shoulders, anywhere I can reach. When I kiss his other nipple, I reach around, tucking my hands in the pockets of his jeans, and pull him in closer to me.

"Samantha." My name is part growl, and part groan. Suddenly, my feet are off the ground, and Tomas is wrapping my legs around his waist. "Bedroom." It's not a question, it's a demand.

"Same direction yours is. I tell him, kissing the side of his neck, and biting his ear. He picks up the pace, and then I'm sailing through the air! I squeal just as I hit the mattress, but I only bounce once, because then the weight of Tomas' body anchors me to the bed.

"I want you so much Samantha, but I have to know that you want this. That you want *me*."

I reach up and caress his cheek. "I want you more than I can possibly express."

"I just don't want you to regret this. After today, my behaviour."

"*Our* behaviour." I correct him, because both of us were in the wrong today. "And I won't regret having sex with you Tomas. Ever."

"You did last time."

"Ohhh baby, I'm sorry I said that to you, I was trying to protect myself, and in the process I hurt you." I pull his lips to mine. "I want you too. I've wanted you since I saw you walk into the bar with Bettie. I was just scared, and for that I'm so, so sorry. I've wasted so much time." I admit.

"I wanted you from the moment Bettie lead me in your direction that night. I couldn't believe my luck when she introduced us." He kisses me possessively, as he steps out of his shoes, and drops his jeans to the floor. He's left standing in front of me in just his boxer briefs, and he's even more amazing than I remember.

"Really? Even with Geri coming on to you, you wanted *me*?" I ask, uncertain. There are few things in this world that I am uncertain about, my being attractive is one of them.

"Geri who? I couldn't see anyone but you. You don't have to believe me, but it's the truth." He pulls me into a sitting position, then he drags my dress up over my head, and tosses it to the floor. "Max spoke to me that night, and told me to be careful with you. He saw it written all over my face before I even realised how deeply I was falling for you." He unfastens my bra, sliding the straps off my shoulders. The bra joins the tangle of clothes on the floor. My underwear joining them not much after, then his do too. I run my hand up and down his cock, and he groans, but that doesn't stop him from running his fingers though my pussy. "Condom. This one is going to be hard, and fast sweetheart." I'm all for that, so I move to reach for the drawer next to my bed. He grabs hold of my wrist, and there's a look on his face that makes me feel like an arsehole.

"They're a new box." I whisper, saying without saying, that I didn't have them here for another man. Not that there would have been for over a year anyway. He drops my wrists, and pulls open the drawer, opens the box himself, tearing a condom from the strip. I lie back on the bed, and just watch him move. I never would have thought that I'd find watching a man roll a condom down his cock could be sexy or sensual, but here I am.

"Move up the bed sweetheart." He demands quietly, but before I can do anything more than lift my butt off the bed, he's picked me up, and then gently places me on my pillows. "Get comfortable. You've got five seconds before I make you mine."

I barely get myself settled, before his body is covering mine again, and he's lining his cock up to enter my body. When just the tip is in, he looks me in the eye. "I am so in love with you, Samantha Holt."

The shock of his confession takes the breath from my lungs, and then he plunges deep into me, taking the rest of my breath, and I wonder if I'll ever breathe again. Slowly he starts pumping in, and out of me.

"Tom." His name is just a breath, my hands are running over every part of his body they can reach. I'm so wound up, from wanting him so badly, to his confession a minute ago, I don't think I'm going to last very long, and that's got to be a first for me. "Tomas!"

"I know. I'm not going to last sweetheart. Next time, I promise." He grounds out between clenched teeth. "I really need you to get there a little faster." He demands, making me chuckle. That is until he reaches between us, and presses his finger against my clit, that quickly has us screaming out each other's names.

He collapses on top of me, resting there for a minute, before pulling out, and taking care of the condom. When he's done, he lies back on the bed, pulls me into his side. I rest my head on his chest, and he kisses my forehead. I couldn't move if I wanted to, and I truly don't want to.

"Did you mean it?" I ask, quietly.

"Every fucking word sweetheart. I am head over heels in love with you, and if you'll have me, I plan on never leaving Sandy Cove, unless I have you by my side." He's lying on his back, one arm wrapped around my shoulder, his eyes closed.

"I love you too, Tomas Jenson." His entire body stiffens, like he wasn't expecting me to admit it yet. "Always."

"Are you sure?" He whispers into the top of my head. "No reservations anymore?"

"Not one. I am head over heels in love with you. I'm sorry I fought it for so long."

"We're here now, and that's what matters." He pulls me tighter into his arms, and know I'm where I'm supposed to be.

Epilogue
18 months later
SAMANTHA

"Oh my word Makenna! This cottage is absolutely gorgeous, I don't know who you got to fix them up, but if the rest of them look like this one, I think you're on a winner hun." I tell Makenna honestly. I know from experience that renovating rundown buildings isn't an easy job.

"My brother, Caleb, was in charge of most of it. He got the builders on board, he had the vision of what he wanted them to be." Makenna beams with pride. "This is the first one that's been completed, so I guess you could say it's the blueprint for the rest."

"Well, I feel honoured that we get to stay in the first one."

"You're popping the cherry, so to speak." Makenna, and I laugh loudly at her joke. "Seriously, if there's anything that you find that's wrong, or that you would change, I would love your feedback. You run a successful resort, so I would appreciate any, and all advice."

"Thank you for the compliment, but I'm sure everything is perfect." I smile, uncomfortable at the compliment.

"I'm sure it's not. Nothing ever is, as you would know. Just know, that at the end of your stay, I want an honest appraisal."

"What do you want an honest appraisal of Makenna?" Tomas' voice rumbles from behind me as he, and Brady walk in the cottage door, making my skin vibrate with an excitement I don't think I'll ever get used to. "I was unaware this was a working holiday." He jokes, as he kisses her on the cheek, and I feel a small amount of jealousy, until he steps closer to me, and pulls me into his front, taking my mouth with his, making me weak at the knees.

"I think we should give them some privacy Makenna." Brady says, kissing his wife on the cheek around the two babies he's carrying.

"Ohhh let me hold the babies!" I squeal, pulling out of Tomas' embrace.

"Wow! Are you sure you wouldn't like me to leave you three alone?" He asks, rolling his eyes at me, all the while smiling broadly.

"They were asleep when we got here, and I want to hold them!" I clap my hands in delight, causing Tomas to roll his eyes again, and Makenna, and Brady to laugh.

"Here, take them, I'm tired of carrying them around." It's my turn to roll my eyes at Brady, because you can see the joy of having his family with him all over his face. They've fought a battle to get here, and I'm so glad they've got the family they wanted so much.

"You love it." I tell him, as I take Anna, and then Beau out of his arms, balancing them on a hip each.

"You're a professional." Makenna beams at me. "Are you sure you can't stay on, and become our nanny?"

I feel Tomas stiffen next to me, like he thinks I might even *think* about staying here, and I laugh. "I'm pretty sure I can't, and won't stay. I'm more than happy at Sandy Cove, I'm not going anywhere, anytime soon. Bettie is talking about actually selling it to us." I smile at Tomas, as he takes Anna from my arms, and cradles her in his arms, smiling down at her cute little face.

"Selling it? Wow that's a huge step for her, she must feel like she's leaving it in great hands with the both of you at the helm." Brady says, tucking Makenna into his side.

"I think you've missed a huge detail here Mr Harris." Makenna says, smacking him on his very tight stomach, and he looks confused. "So, the *two* of you huh? Does that mean this thing between you two is serious?" She asks, her eyes darting between the two of us, a huge smile on her face.

Tomas looks away from Anna to look at me, a twinkle in his eyes, and I see the unconditional love there. Love I wish I hadn't fought for so damned long, he smiles at me, and I tell Makenna the absolute truth.

"Yes." I look away from his handsome face to see Makenna absolutely beaming at me. Suddenly she's crushing me in her arms, and bouncing around in happiness.

"Sorry baby." She says quietly, kissing Beau on the top of his head as he grumbles quietly about being shuffled about. "I'm so happy for you both."

"She resisted for a while, but I wore her down eventually." Tomas says, and then he's the one engulfed in Makenna's embrace. "I, ummm actually proposed to her just before we left home." He looks at me, love is all I see on his face, and I can't help hating that I wasted so much time worrying about what other people would think if we got together.

"What?!" Makenna squeals, making both babies jump, and start to cry. As if on cue their uncles, Makenna's brothers, Logan, and Caleb, appear out of nowhere and take the babies out of our arms. Caleb taking Beau from me, and Logan delivering Anna into his own arms so efficiently from Tomas', I can't help wondering how many times he's done it before. With both men cooing at the babies, Makenna is free to hug us both tightly once again. "Oh, hang on. Did she say yes?" She asks, stepping back to look between us both.

"Yes." I say quietly.

"Yeah, she did." Tomas says, taking my hand in his, and pulling me close.

"Show me." Makenna demands, and Tomas blushes.

"There isn't a ring. Yet." I say in a rush.

"I was planning on proposing, and getting the ring while we were here, but one thing lead to another, and I asked her before we left." Tomas says in a rush.

"We know an amazing jeweller, don't we Brady?" Makenna says excitedly.

"Calm down baby. They can choose their own ring, and jeweller." Brady says, pulling his wife into his arms, smiling indulgently at her.

"I know but, oh my god I'm so happy for you both. I knew it. Didn't I tell you Brady? I told you these two were in love with each other they were just too stubborn to admit it when we were there."

"Well, to be fair it was like they were in *lust*, while we were at Sandy Cove, but yes, you were absolutely right in your prediction that they would get together." Brady acknowledges with a smile. "Congratulations guys, that's amazing." He reaches out a hand to Tomas, who takes it, and they shake.

"Thanks Brady."

"Right well, we'll get out of your hair. I'll have dinner sent to the room, just let Leila know at Vines, what time you want it." She starts to leave the cottage. "Come on, everyone out, let's leave these two alone so that they can celebrate their engagement. Alone, if you get my meaning."

"Why Kenna? Just why do you have to put those kinds of images into my head. You should be more careful now, you've got young children to consider here." Caleb complains.

"Just get out of the cottage Caleb, and then you won't have worry about it at all." Logan commands.

"But it's already in my head now." Caleb whines, but moves towards the door, Logan right behind him.

"That's your own fault man. If you had a cleaner mind, you wouldn't have to ask everyone else around you to filter what they say, or do. Now move." Logan follows Caleb out the door, almost pushing him forward.

"I see what you mean now man." Tomas says, slapping Brady on the back as they walk to the door. Brady just grunts in response, and Makenna rolls her eyes. I have no clue what's going on, but I'll ask Tomas once everyone has left.

"Come on, let's get home, feed these monsters, then they can help us feed Anna and Beau." I laugh realising what Makenna said. "Trust me, my brothers are the real children in our world, the babies are fantastic."

"They are beautiful Makenna, I'm so happy for you both." I tell her, giving her a warm hug at the door.

"Me too. We'll talk more in the morning. Go back inside and enjoy some time with your man. Your *fiancé*!"

"I will." I reply, blushing a deep red.

We say our goodbyes multiple times before finally closing the door behind everyone.

"Are you upset I told them?" Tomas asks, pulling me in his embrace, and kissing my forehead.

I kiss the side of this neck lightly, and I feel a shiver run through him. "I don't mind at all." I say, kissing him again, then sucking on his skin gently.

"Fuck." He mutters.

"Want to christen the new cottage?" I ask, my voice raspy.

"If you think Caleb hasn't beaten us to it already, you're kidding yourself, but I definitely want to have sex with you in every room. I'll just tell Brady he has to disinfect the place after we leave."

"You're terrible." I say, while laughing with my lips still resting against his throat.

"But you know you love me." He says, running his hands under top, and un-hooking my bra in one swift move.

"I do."

"I can't wait for you to say that in front of a celebrant." He murmurs as his lips travel across my bare shoulder.

"Me either, but first, a ring mister."

"First thing tomorrow, I promise."

His promise is good enough for me. It wasn't for a long time, and I am constantly mad at myself for all the time I wasted, but Tomas doesn't hold it against me. He assures me that he'd rather I be one hundred percent onboard with our relationship, than second guessing it at every point.

"You're worth waiting for." I say quietly in his ear, repeating what he's always telling *me,* and I feel the smile spread across his lips on my skin. "I love you Tomas Jenson."

"I love you, Samantha Holt. Always."

DRAKE WINES SERIES

VINEYARD - Book .1.
SANDY COVE – A novella
(to be read after Vineyard)
~~*OUT SOON*~*~*
WINERY - Book .2.
LORI'S MEMORIES – A novella
(to be read after Winery)
BREWERY - Book .3.
SARA'S FOREVER – A novella
(to be read after Brewery)
AVAILABLE ON:
KINDLE
APPLE
KOBO
GOOGLE PLAY
BARNES & NOBLE
AND AS PAPERBACKS

Other books by

Chelle Pimblott
SNEAKY LOVE SERIES
SNEAKY Book .1.
SNEAKING AROUND – Book .2.
NO MORE SNEAKING AROUND – Book .3.
BUILT FOR LOVE SERIES
BUILT TO LAST – Book .1.
BUILT FOR TROUBLE – Book .2.
A STANDALONE
BAREFOOT & DUMPED!
AVAILABLE ON:
KINDLE
APPLE
KOBO
GOOGLE PLAY
BARNES & NOBLE
AND AS PAPERBACKS

YOU CAN CHELLE PIMBLOTT ON:

FACEBOOK
GOODREADS
AMAZON
TWITTER
INSTAGRAM

Don't miss out!

Visit the website below and you can sign up to receive emails whenever Chelle pimblott publishes a new book. There's no charge and no obligation.

https://books2read.com/r/B-A-FGVL-BCFOB

BOOKS 2 READ

Connecting independent readers to independent writers.

Also by Chelle pimblott

Built for Love
Built to Last
Built for Trouble

Drake Wines
Vineyard
Sandy Cove - A Drake Wines Novella
Winery

Standalone
Barefoot & Dumped!